# MEDUSA'S SON

## IAN MITCHELL-GILL

This is a work of fiction. Names, characters, places, and incidents are products of the author's imagination or are used fictitiously and are not to be construed as real. Any resemblance to actual events, locations, organizations, or persons, living or dead, is entirely coincidental.

**World Castle Publishing, LLC**
Pensacola, Florida
Copyright © 2024 Ian Mitchell-Gill
Paperback ISBN: 9798891261266
eBook ISBN: 9798891261273
First Edition World Castle Publishing, LLC, February 14, 2024
http://www.worldcastlepublishing.com
**Licensing Notes**
Cover: Cover Designs by Karen
https://www.cover-designs-by-karen.com
Editor: Karen Fuller

This book is dedicated to the loving memory of:
Myron Caky
1970-2019
Friend, uncle, brother, son.
Taken far too soon.

# CHAPTER 1

I've heard it said that secrets will be the end of us, but I say they can be a beginning. At least it was for me.

I remember the lights. So many lights. Pulsing, flashing in every color. Dancers moved on the floor in the artificial smoke and the smog they had produced themselves.

There were nightclubs, and there were nightclubs. The Dancing Duck was a whole other level of hedonism. I looked left and right at all the beautiful Russians dancing with abandon and making out on the outskirts of the dance floor. They partied like it was their last night on earth, and in this mafia-run city, it really could be.

I was leaning against a black wall, taking it all in. It was the most fun I'd had since my father took the job in the American Embassy in Russia, and I had to leave college. I dressed in a nice black shirt and a decent pair of jeans. No jewelry, as I didn't want to show any level of wealth or call attention to myself in any way. My dad's interpreter told us not to identify ourselves as a mark to the locals. He also told us not to go out alone. Didn't follow that bit of advice. Where's the fun in that?

I felt eyes on me and turned to see a tall redhead looking at me with a smile on her ruby lips. Our eyes locked, and I looked away. Dammit! *Why did I do that?*

Looking at my shoes as I ran my hand through my hair, I was hating myself for punking out yet again. When I looked back, she was gone. I blew it. I can never seem to look back when someone is giving me the eye. It's not that I'm not attracted to women. I am…believe me. It's just hard for me to return that smile. I always feel caught when I make eye contact with a pretty girl. What the hell is wrong with me?

I felt a touch on my arm, and she was there. Her green eyes burned into mine, and she was wearing a smile…*and what a smile*. Like she knew me or wanted to.

She leaned in to speak into my ear. "You are American, yes? Alone, no?" she purred with that smooth Moscow accent.

"Yes, yes! How did you know?" I asked.

Again, the killer smile before she leaned in to speak again. "Your haircut, it is the latest style. You look everywhere. This is all new for you, yes?"

I laughed and ran a hand through my hair. My stylist had talked me into blond highlights at the tips of my light-brown hair. Said it would make my blue eyes "pop." Maybe she was right. Something was happening for me this night.

"Elena," she said, pointing at herself. Then she pointed at me and raised an eyebrow.

"W-Walt. I'm Walt," I stammered back, looking right down at the daring plunge in her little black dress. That amazing cleavage was on display...but that didn't make it right to stare. I hated myself for that.

She looked down at her chest, back at me, and her smile grew. Elena put her hands on my shoulders and started rocking her hips in a seductive little dance. "Move with me, Walt," she commanded with a sly grin.

"We're not on the dance floor."

Elena tilted her head toward me. "Nobody cares. Why should you?" She leaned very close, and I felt her breath in my ear. "I like you, Walt."

I didn't fight her as she moved me towards a dark corner. I didn't know what she had in mind, but I liked where this was going. I moved with her, and we got to the corner, right by a black door you could barely make out in the dark.

She turned herself to put her back against the door and ran her hands down my chest as she danced. She was really turning me on. Her green eyes seemed to almost glow in the gloom of the corner.

I stared into her eyes. They didn't look normal. Contacts? I was thinking about asking her, but I never got the chance.

She smirked as she looked over my shoulder and then pulled hard as she backed through the door, bringing us both out into the cold Moscow night. Her heels and my shoes crunched in the snow as she pressed my back against the brick wall of the alley.

"Elena! What are you doing?" I asked, gasping as I felt the cold air through my shirt. I started moving forward, but she pushed me back into the wall. She was stronger than she looked.

She launched into me, and I felt her lips on my neck. Talk about aggressive! But all that changed when she nipped me. "OW!" I shouted and pushed her back, hard. My hand instinctively went to my neck, and it felt warm and sticky. I pulled my hand back in front of my face and saw a smear of blood. "What the hell, Elena!" I shouted at her. My mouth hung open when I saw her face.

Elena's eyes were burning like they were green fire, but it was her mouth that shocked me the most. It was huge, and pointy teeth pushed out at the corners. Her tongue was hanging out and swollen. Her hands darted to her neck, and she made a choking sound as blood poured out of her nose and ears.

I moved down the wall to get away from her. Still, she continued to struggle to breathe, and her skin seemed to be boiling below the surface. She fell to her knees, and the flesh fell away from her skull. Seconds later, there was just red sludge on a blackened skeleton wearing a black dress in the snow.

I turned to the door and tried to get back into the club, but it had locked behind me. Elena knew what she was doing. She'd pulled me into that alley, and when the door closed, I had nowhere else to go. But what happened to her?

"Hey!" I heard from the end of the alley. Two Moscow policemen with guns strapped around their shoulders were marching toward me.

# CHAPTER 2

Not how I thought this night was going to go. Sure, I was hoping to have a few drinks, take in the sights, and maybe even meet a nice Russian girl. I wouldn't have even minded if the night was a dead loss. You never can tell.

But I never thought I'd find myself chained to a chair in some bureaucrat's office. It was a nice chair and a nice office. A red carpet on the floor and dark wood furniture gave the place an air of class. There was a brass nametag on the desk beside a sharp-looking letter opener. It read, "I. Kamenev."

Getting to this point had been quite a ride. The Russian cops arrested me and were none too gentle about it. They didn't speak English at all, so there was no communication. I had to sit in a freezing police car while they examined what was left of poor Elena.

Seemed like an eternity before another car arrived with a superior officer. After that, things happened fast. The new guy ran to the car and got a shovel and a garbage bag. Should I be concerned that Russian cops keep a shovel and a garbage bag in their cars?

Anyway, he gave it to the cops who'd arrested me and marched over to the car. He opened the door, and I felt the cold rush in. He had dark eyes and a heavy brow. "You are American?" he barked at me.

"Yes."

He pointed a beefy hand at me and then towards the alley. "How did you kill girl?"

"I didn't! She bit me, and then...then she did that." I turned my head to show him the wound on my neck.

His eyes opened wide when he saw my neck. He slammed the door and jogged back to the cops, cleaning up the mess. One of them was leaning against the wall, puking.

The big guy reached into the bag and picked out the blackened skull. I felt the taste of bile in my mouth and thought I was going to barf, too.

He showed the skull to the other cop, and they both looked at each other. Something remained unsaid between them. The cop turned and spat on the snow as his superior rammed the skull into the bag. What was bothering them?

Beefy, the supervisor, opened my door and pulled me out, steadying me on the slippery road. He was taller than I thought. He walked me over to his car and put me in the back. He left, then came back with my coat. He made me lean forward and draped the coat over my shoulders. I was starting to like this guy.

He sat down in the driver's seat, and I felt the whole car sag. We drove for about twenty minutes. All I saw were the dark streets and fat snowflakes hitting the window. We stopped at a big building, and he escorted me up the stairs and through the lobby. We got into an ancient elevator, and he had to close the door by hand. Rising to the top floor, neither of us said a word.

I thought things were looking good when we entered the nice office. That is until he chained my handcuffs to the chair and left. Hours passed, and I was starting to see the dawn through one of the windows.

Finally, I heard the creak of the door, and a man in a suit carrying a piece of paper walked to the desk and sat down. He had black hair that was slicked back, keeping it neat. I pegged him at being in his early sixties. His blue suit was immaculate, and he had a red star as a lapel pin.

His dark eyes stared into mine, unblinking. His mouth barely opened as he spoke. "You are Walt." He glanced at the paper in front of him. "Walter Baranov, are you not?"

The man's English was excellent, and it was a relief to hear. "Yes! What the hell is happening?"

"You were found beside a body, a girl. Outside the Dancing Duck." He took a breath and narrowed his eyes. "Tell me how she died."

I squirmed in my seat and showed him my neck. "She pulled me into the alley, and the freak actually bit me!"

"And then?" There was no emotion in his voice. His focus was intense.

"I have no idea! Her eyes started glowing green, and blood started pouring out of her eyes and mouth." My lips started shaking, reliving it again. "She kind of melted away."

The man gave a slight nod and raised an eyebrow. "Did her mouth change in any way after she bit you?"

I took a breath and let it out slowly. "Oh, yeah! It was bigger and full of sharp teeth. Totally gross."

He leaned forward and pressed a button on his desk. A woman walked in wearing a blue skirt and blazer and had the same red star on her lapel as her boss. Her dark hair was swept back into a ponytail. Her glasses had thick frames. He spoke to her in Russian, and she nodded, turned on her heel, and left.

My inquisitor rose out of his seat and came to my chair. I could hear the chime of keys in his hand and felt the chain tighten as he worked to free me. "My name is Ivan Kamenev. I must apologize for the way you were apprehended. This is something we have never seen before, and my men were uncertain about how to proceed."

The woman returned with a black bag, and he

gestured her over toward me. "Svetlana will apply a dressing to that wound on your neck. It must be sterilized, and I'm afraid the bleeding will start again before she applies the bandage."

"Okay, thank you for that," I mumbled before Svetlana's strong hands grabbed my head and tilted it to access my neck. I winced as she applied some ointment, and she quickly slapped some gauze on the injury. I could feel that it had started bleeding again.

Kamenev had returned to his desk, and he sat down with a sigh. "Why did you go to the Dancing Duck last night?"

I shrugged. "I heard it was a wild party. I wanted to see it for myself. Have you ever been?"

His mouth moved into what I guessed was a smile. "A place for a younger man. Had you ever seen the woman you identify as Elena before that night?"

"No, never."

He said something to Svetlana, and she asked a question in return. He nodded his head, and she turned and strutted from the room. He looked at me. "Very well, Walt. Svetlana is going to make us tea. Is there anything you require?"

"One thing, Mr. Kamenev, can I please use a washroom? I've been chained to a chair for hours."

He stood up quickly and gestured behind him. "You may use my personal bathroom. When you finish, I will explain it all."

# CHAPTER 3

The bathroom was simple, clean, and a huge relief. I was worried I wasn't going to make it! I washed and dried my hands on a plush red hand towel and looked in the mirror at the tired guy staring back at me.

I ran a hand through my medium-length brown hair to move it into place or at least look better than it did. The blond highlights looked weird in the light. My eyes were blue and paler than normal. It was strange, but the more tired I got, the paler they got. "What did you get yourself into this time?" I asked myself.

I walked back into Kamenev's office and back to the chair that had been my prison until recently. I'd just sat down when the efficient Svetlana made her way back in with the tea on a tray. It was simple but elegant chinaware, with gold painted on the delicate handles. There were some slices of lemon, sugar, a couple of spoons, and a mason jar with steaming water in the middle. I wasn't sure what the mason jar was for.

Kamenev gestured toward the tea. "Please, help yourself."

I took the cup closest to me, added some lemon, and gave it a sip. "Very nice, thanks. Mr. Kamenev, I've got to call my parents and tell them I'm okay."

The man nodded and helped himself to his own cup. He added nothing but blew and drew a quick drink. "We will speak of your parents later. We called them last night and let them know your whereabouts." He let out the slightest of sighs and tented his fingers on the desk. "Do you understand what is happening here? Do you know who that young woman was?"

I set down my tea and shrugged. "I know she said her name was Elena, and she was beautiful. Now she's dead. That's it."

He raised an eyebrow. "She was much more than she appeared and less." He sat back in his chair and turned slightly, looking out the window. "She was a vampire, Walt."

I looked at the man and frowned. Did I hear that right? "Are...are you trying to be funny? Or is that some Russian expression I don't understand?"

Kamenev snorted a small laugh. "I don't blame you. I understand how this must sound. But it is true."

It was my turn to sit back in the chair. "You're not seriously going to try and tell me that vampires are real?"

The Russian shrugged. "I didn't believe it either. Until I lost my wife and daughter to the damnable virus."

"Virus? Okay, I'm lost. We were just talking about vampires, and now we're talking about a virus."

"One and the same. That young woman was once like you. She probably went to nightclubs for the same reason you did. She went for very different reasons last night."

I shook my head. "Things were going fine until she…" I couldn't finish the sentence.

"Until she bit you."

"Okay, that's true." I reached for my tea. Kamenev sat impassively while I was trying to digest this madness. Then I had it. "Vampires don't die after they bite someone. She didn't even get any blood. It was one chomp, and she just…you know."

"Disintegrated."

I sipped the tea and nodded. "Yeah. How does that make her a vampire?" I set down the cup and swallowed. "You're actually trying to tell me that vampires are real?"

He tapped a finger on his desk. "Think about this, Walt. She probably made sure you were alone and then maneuvered you into that alley. Nobody to see, nobody to help you. You were the perfect victim. For her, an opportunity to feed."

This guy was making more sense than I liked. "Wow…well, that's what happened. But why did she die?"

He leaned forward, and his elbows rested on

the desk. "That is an excellent question." His eyes narrowed as he looked at my neck. "Your dressing needs changing, I think." He pressed the button on his desk, and Svetlana returned. She was none too gentle removing the bandage, and I thought it was weird that she dropped the blood-stained gauze in the mason jar with the water before putting on a new dressing.

Kamenev finished his tea. "I am wasting my time with words. Perhaps you must see for yourself."

***

We were heading toward the ancient elevator, and Kamenev was carrying the mason jar that held my old bandage. The water had turned a little pink as the blood mixed. He was talking as we got on. "It is not common knowledge, Walt. Vampires hide in the shadows of many countries. They are very careful in their secrecy. It is everything to them."

"Do the leaders of the country know about this? I mean, how do you keep a secret like this?"

The Russian shrugged as he closed the door to the rickety old elevator. "It's not hard. The creatures hide themselves. Government officials can easily conceal a victim. It is particularly easy in a country like the United States."

"What do you mean?"

The elevator started down, and he raised his voice to be heard. "It's an easy matter to shoot someone in the wound that a vampire has inflicted. Gun violence is not rare in your country." He looked at me with a quick glance. "I know your father is part of the American Embassy. I mean no disrespect."

"None taken."

The elevator went down and down. It got dark, and when we came to a stop, the hallway looked much more modern. There was one thick steel door at the end of the corridor. Kamenev opened the elevator door, and the two of us walked down the corridor. He reached into his pocket and pulled out a heavy steel key. He rammed it in the lock, turned it, and there was an audible click. He yanked open the door to this vault.

He gestured for me to enter. I did not want to go first. But what could I do? I took a couple of baby steps through the door. It smelled awful. Dank and rotten. About ten steps in, I could see the door to a cell. A jail.

Kamenev walked past me and said something loudly in Russian. I could hear some hissing, but I still couldn't see anyone. The Russian escorting me looked my way. "Do not get too close, okay?"

I nodded. He needn't have worried. I didn't like any of this, and nothing could get me near the door of that cell. I couldn't see anything in the dark corners of that prison.

"HEY!" Kamenev barked into the darkness. He reached into a steel box by the wall, drew out a red, rubbery bag, and threw it into the cell.

Out of nowhere, this big, naked, and filthy shape leapt out of the corner and grabbed the bag with long, clawed fingers. It was bald, with a few long, stringy black hairs plastered to the filth of its scalp. It jammed the bag into its toothy maw, and blood dripped out of the corners of its mouth onto the floor. When it was done feeding, it looked at us with glowing green eyes and gave a threatening hiss of hatred.

Kamenev scowled at it. "Walt, this is Yuri. He has been here for some time."

The creature looked at me, and I thought I heard it laugh. *"Kamenev, ya tebya nenavizhu!"* it spat out in Russian.

"He doesn't like me," Kamenev deadpanned.

I didn't know what to say. My mouth was hanging open, and I was just staring. It was impossible, and there it was. An honest-to-God vampire. It was horrible, and it was fascinating.

The thing jumped at the bars, and I yelped and took a few steps back behind my host. "This...this is crazy!" I whispered to Kamenev as I cowered behind him.

"Yes. It is madness, I know. But there it is. Walt, I did not believe in such things myself. Until this thing came to my home and took my wife and child from me." His face darkened as he looked at the monster. "And now I have taken everything from him. I have one more thing to take."

"So there really are vampires," I whispered. "But what killed Elena?"

The creature snapped its head to look me right in the eyes. It looked right through me. *"Elena!"* it hissed and then laughed.

Kamenev took the mason jar with the bloody dressing and unscrewed the lid. The creature started sniffing and reached out for it. Kamenev threw it at the creature and stepped back into me.

The disgusting thing took a step back, too, and started clawing at its face. Pustules of blood formed on its skin and exploded in pink clouds as it gave a gurgling scream. The skin sloughed off its skull, and soon, the rest of the flesh followed it to the floor. All that was left was a red and grey puddle of bones steaming on the floor.

Kamenev shook his head slowly and turned to look at me. "Elena was a vampire, Walt. What killed her...was biting you."

# CHAPTER 4

"So now you know," Kamenev said as he sealed the large steel door. "That was one of many."

My hands were still shaking. I couldn't get the image of that horrible thing dying out of my mind. "How many are there?"

Kamenev shrugged. "There is no way to know."

"What *do* you know?

We got on to the elevator, and the Russian closed the door. He spoke louder to be heard over the clatter of the ancient contraption. "We know they have infiltrated every major city in the world. Some more than others. They have a complex social and political hierarchy. Most of their communication takes place in secret locations and the dark web."

Arriving at our floor, he wrenched open the creaky door and gestured for me to exit first. We walked down the hall towards his office. "That thing in the cell didn't look anything like the poor woman I met at the club," I said.

"He was very old. At least two hundred years. The woman was nowhere near that age."

I couldn't believe what I was hearing. "They get *that* old?"

"Even older."

When we walked into his office, I was surprised to see Svetlana setting a new tray with some cookies as well. Kamenev said something in Russian to her, and she smiled ear to ear. She walked up to me and gave me a gentle hug. I froze. She gave me a kiss on each cheek, and there were tears in her eyes as she stepped back and regarded me. "Spasibo," she whispered and left the room.

Kamenev was wearing a small smile and gestured for me to sit. "What was that all about?" I asked.

"She is celebrating," the man answered as he poured tea for each of us. "So am I."

When we were both sitting with a warm drink in our hands, I couldn't contain myself any longer. "I have a lot of questions."

"No doubt. Ask me anything."

"Okay, how long have these things been around?"

He took a breath and let it out slowly. "That's a question without a certain answer. The first reported vampire in Europe was Jure Grando in 1656. He lived in a small village named Kringa, located in Croatia.

There are mentions of creatures drinking blood as far back as the ancient Babylonians, but nothing verified. We cannot know for sure when this started."

"Are the stories true?"

He raised an eyebrow slightly. "Which ones?

"Oh, you know...sleeping in coffins, afraid of the daylight and garlic."

Kamenev took a sip of his tea and swallowed. "They sleep in beds like everybody. Daylight does them no harm. The old ones avoid the light because of their appearance and the fear of being discovered. Imagine that monster in the basement walking through Red Square. How would that turn out?"

It made sense. "And garlic?"

He smirked. "The things drink blood. Why would they want or need garlic? They generally don't like strong smells of any kind, as their senses are so keen. It does not repel them in any way."

That wasn't very comforting. "But they die if you cut off their heads or drive a stake through their heart...right?"

He shrugged. "Everything dies if you cut off the head or smash a piece of wood through the heart."

The man had a point. "Yeah, I see what you mean. What was that liquid you used to kill that vampire in the basement?"

All humor drained away from his face, and he looked me right in the eyes. "It was a tincture of warm water and your blood."

My eyes opened wide. "Nothing else?"

He shook his head, watching my face as I pieced it together.

"You're saying my blood killed that thing?"

The Russian pointed at me. "Two known vampires have come in physical contact with you, and both died immediately."

I shook my head. "That's not true. The woman in the club was all over me before she died in that alley."

His eyes narrowed. "Did she actually touch you in the club? Or did she merely handle your clothing? Did her skin touch yours?"

It hit me hard, and I sat back in the chair. "No. She didn't actually touch me before we went into the alley."

"You're starting to see my point. Walt, something about you causes vampires to die the moment they come into contact with your blood."

I set my teacup down. I wasn't thirsty, and my mind was racing. "But why?"

"That is a question that must be answered." He looked at his watch. "We leave for Japan within the hour."

"Japan! Whoa!" I held up both my hands to slow this cowboy down. "My parents are never going to go for that. I can tell you that right now."

Kamenev linked his fingers on the desk and tilted his head toward me. "Your parents were on the first plane out of Moscow about two hours after you were arrested. For their safety, you understand."

I didn't. "Why would their safety be jeopardized by any of this? It has nothing to do with them."

"The wrong people will eventually know what happened in that alley. It's just a matter of time. They will try to eliminate anyone involved. Killing your parents would just be standard procedure."

I put my hands together in my lap and leaned forward in the chair. "What do you mean by 'wrong people,' exactly?"

The Russian frowned at me. "Use your head! When it is discovered that there is a young man whose existence is deadly to vampires, killing you will become a priority for a great many people. Vampires protect their interests, and there are ordinary people who are in league with these devils." He looked down and shook his head slowly. "Walt, whatever it is that makes you deadly to these creatures makes you a threat that needs to be eliminated."

Woah, woah, woah, did he just say kill me!? I had to think fast before panic set in. I felt the blood drain from my face, and I swallowed. "Couldn't I just go back to the States? I'm sure I could just disappear. Like a witness protection program or something."

Kamenev's eyes softened. "You would be safe...for a time. And then you would be dead and incinerated. They will find you."

"So I should go to Japan?"

"Yes. If we can find out what is causing this phenomenon, perhaps we can synthesize it. Use it in a way to stamp out these vermin. Then, there would be no reason to eliminate you. It would be pointless."

I looked at my shoes. "I think I get it now. My parents are okay with this?"

"They are. Our American counterparts have explained the situation. They are not pleased, but they understand." He stood up and looked down at me. "It is time to go."

Standing with him, I shrugged. "Okay, wow. Japan. Why Japan?"

He walked toward the door and gestured for me to follow. "I will explain on the flight. It's around nine hours, so we have time. Come, my young friend."

# CHAPTER 5

We grabbed our coats and headed for the lobby. Kamenev took me to a car in the parking lot, and I guessed it was his own. Just a plain, black, boxy thing. He wasn't rushing me, but he didn't dawdle either. The man guided the car down the snowy roads smoothly, a small smile on his lips. "Svetlana lost her husband and two sons to that disgusting vampire you met."

"I'm sorry," was all I could manage as I watched the road.

"She has dedicated her life to the destruction of these miserable creatures. She is a good woman. A tireless worker. I think knowing you exist and that your blood destroyed that monster has awakened something in her."

"What?"

He stole a quick glance at me and then turned back to the road. "Hope. I think she has hope that nobody else will suffer what the rest of the division has had to endure."

The car pulled sharply into an airfield. We stopped at a guard checkpoint, where Kamenev identified himself and was waved through quickly. He never told me his title or position, but it was clear that he ranked high. Very high.

When we got to the plane, I recognized the beefy police officer who had driven me to Kamenev's building and chained me to the chair. He was standing there, impassive as ever, but held a suitcase in his hand. My suitcase.

My driver cleared his throat. "Officer Volkov was instructed to gather things from your room for your journey. He only took a few things and some toiletries. We will provide you with anything you need when you reach your destination."

The car came to a stop, and we got out. Kamenev gestured at the burly police officer who took a couple of steps toward me, holding out my bag. "Udachi tebe," he said between tight lips and clapped me on the shoulder as I took the bag. He unslung a machine gun from his shoulder and turned away from me, scanning the airfield.

Kamenev took my arm and guided me away from the car. We started walking toward a sleek and sharp-looking blue Learjet. I saw numbers and unusual characters near the door. The stairs came down, and a man wearing a white shirt with gold epaulets and a black tie waved. The Russian beside me shouted,

"Junbi kanyro," with a flawless Japanese accent. I heard the jets fire up. It wasn't the only thing I heard.

A strange popping sound could be heard far away. I saw Kamenev frown, and the big officer Volkov started running in the direction of the sound, gun in hand. "What is that?" I asked.

"That is the distinct sound of a Kalashnikov. A very effective Russian machine gun. It's time we left. You are no longer a secret, Walt."

He hustled me up the gangway, and the man in the white shirt was gesturing for us to sit down as he hauled up the stairs and closed the door. I'd barely gotten in the nice brown leather chair, Kamenev across from me, when the jet started moving. The pilot wasn't messing around. We taxied fast to the runway and blasted off as soon as we turned the plane. I felt the strong engines pushing us forward, and the force made me sink back into the soft seat. We were airborne.

Kamenev got up when the seatbelt sign went off. "I am getting a drink. Would you like one?"

"What are you having?"

He shrugged. "Vodka, naturally."

I couldn't help laughing. "I'm not really a drinker. A bottle of water would be great."

The man snorted a laugh and moved toward the front of the plane. I looked out the window. The morning sun was bright, and the clouds looked soft and were pure white. It wasn't comforting. I had no idea what was waiting for me at the end of this flight.

The Russian came back with a bottle of water for me and a tumbler full of ice and vodka for his own refreshment. He tossed the drink my way, and I had to scramble to catch it. The man dropped into his seat and let out a big sigh before he took a belt of the alcohol. "It is early, but I am celebrating."

"That's the second time you've said that. What is the occasion?"

He held the glass up in a salute. "Finding you. Finding something that would change everything forever."

I opened the water and took a drink as my Russian companion took a serious swig of the vodka. He wasn't new to the drink. I raised a hand. "So now we can talk?"

Kamenev gestured for me to start. "Anything. We can start wherever you like."

"Okay, cool. Right. Vampires are real, but it's a big secret. How have you been able to keep a lid on this?"

"It has not been hard. Do you have any idea how many unsolved homicides there are in the world? Do you know how many there are in the United States alone? Well over fifteen thousand. I'm not saying that vampires are responsible for all of them, but they become unsolved when it is confirmed that it is a person who fell prey to one of those fiends."

I nodded as it sank in. "And like you said, you can always fire a gun into the telltale wound, am I right?"

He swirled the ice around in his glass and smirked at me. "You listen well. Vampires themselves hide their existence. They feed on animal blood, and we believe they can synthesize the plasma that they need. Any of their members who flagrantly kill and do not cover their tracks are destroyed by their own kind. They do have ordinary people who are paid well to help meet their needs and keep the truth hidden. It is a large and evil network."

I pointed a finger at him. "How do you kill these things? The legends and folktales are all wrong, but there must be some way."

Kamenev laughed. "The legends are very wrong. Removing the head seems to do an effective job. However, if they can feed after being mortally wounded, it seems to help them heal and survive. They are difficult to destroy."

"You did say it was a virus, right?"

He frowned and looked down at his glass. It was nearly empty. "That...that seems like an oversimplification. It certainly is a virus, but it is more than that. It destroys the person's ability to manufacture their own blood cells, and like rabies, it can affect their mental state. The kindest soul becomes a merciless slave to the never-ending thirst. A predator who lures innocents to their deaths or attacks when it senses vulnerability."

I sat back in my chair and took a drink from my

bottle. Kamenev took the opportunity to get up and move back to the bar. Was he really pouring himself another vodka?

He came back to his seat, and his glass was nearly full. "Keep asking. It is rare that I can talk about such things."

I hesitated to ask what had been on my mind since I met him. Seemed a little personal, but what the hell. "How did you get involved in all this? Why are you in on the secret?"

The Russian ran a hand through his hair and laughed. "There was no keeping this secret from me. I was moving up the ranks as a police officer, and I came home to find one of these monsters in my house. I shot it full of bullets, and I was able to capture Yuri, the thing you met in the cell." He grew quiet, and I saw him clench his jaw. "I was too late to be any good to my wife and daughter. He had already taken them." The glass came to his mouth, and he took a big drink. "And that is why I am celebrating."

"I...I'm sorry for what happened to your family." It was all I could think to say. An awkward silence followed. What do you say to a man who lost his family to a monster?

He shrugged and snorted a laugh. The vodka was working. "It is in the past, and that is where I leave it. The high command was pleased with my actions, and I have dedicated my life to destroying these beasts. It has brought me purpose, but it has not brought me peace."

"And you think something about me is going to help you kill the vampires in the world?"

He looked me dead in the eyes, and his mouth was grim. "You have seen it for yourself. Two vampires were touched by your blood, and two vampires are dead because of that contact. This could completely change the balance of power. Another reason I celebrate!"

I took a drink of my water, and Kamenev brought up his glass for another swig of the alcohol. I looked at him and shrugged. "Do you ever feel sorry for them?"

"What?" He stared at me, unsure of what his ears were telling him.

I held up my hands. "Well, I mean...I know it's dumb, but if these people are infected by a kind of virus that makes them crazy and dangerous..."

He sat forward in his chair, looking at me with narrowed eyes. "You feel pity for them?"

I looked at the floor. "I know it's stupid. But Elena was so beautiful and so full of life. I know she meant to make a meal of me, but she used to have a normal life, and that was probably taken from her. I know you probably think I'm an idiot, but there's a part of me that feels sorry for her. For what happened to her."

I felt the Russian's hand on my knee, and I was surprised to see tears in his eyes when I looked up. "No, Walt. I do not think you are an idiot. I think you are good and kind. The other reason I am celebrating is that Elena is at peace." He sat back and held up his glass in a toast. "She was my wife."

# CHAPTER 6

"Your wife?! But she was so young, beautiful, and you're, uh…not."

Kamenev let out a braying belly laugh. "I like you, Walt. I never know what you will say next." He laughed some more and wiped a tear away as he continued. "I was much younger when Elena was turned. I aged, and she did not."

"Oh, of course. I should have known. I'm so sorry that she died like that."

The Russian waved a dismissive hand. "She was lost to me a long time ago. That creature had Elena's beauty but no heart." He leaned forward and clasped my knee again. "I am glad she is finally at rest."

I felt a little less awkward about the whole thing. "I guess that's one way of looking at it."

"It is the *only* way to look at it." He got up and fished a couple of blue blankets and some pillows from the overhead storage bin. "Here, rest, Walt. Sleep, if you can."

Without another word, he drained his glass and reclined in his chair. A moment later, he was asleep. I guess the vodka and the deaths of Elena and Yuri took it all out of him.

I put a pillow behind my head and spread a blanket on my front. I closed my eyes, but sleep wouldn't come. I kept picturing the death of Elena and that ghastly creature, Yuri. Horrible!

Oh sure, I had no choice in the matter. But knowing that something about me had killed them was enough to keep me awake. I didn't want anyone to die because of me. But if monsters died, that was a good thing...right? It didn't feel right. Maybe I was just tired.

Sleep must have come at some point because I jerked awake when I felt the plane start to descend. We drifted through the clouds, and I saw the coast of Japan and the majestic Mount Fuji. It was beautiful! We were coming down in a hurry. Did the pilot want to land on the beach?

We did touch down on a runway, and it was pretty smooth. I guess they don't let just anyone fly such an awesome jet. Kamenev stirred and blinked. "Ah! We are here. We have arrived at Haneda."

The plane taxied to a standstill, and I saw a long, black car drive out to meet us. My Russian escort grabbed my bag, and the pilots came out and dealt with the door and the steps to exit the plane. They stood shoulder to shoulder. Two Japanese pilots were not looking directly at me, but they were kind of staring at me. Staring but not staring.

Kamenev gestured at the exit, brightened by the sun, and I started walking. The two pilots bent at the waist in a formal bow and held it. It was almost touching.

I glued my hands to my sides and returned the gesture with a bow of my own. Kamenev joined me, and they all waited for me to straighten out first. Took me a moment to figure that out!

When I stood tall, they stood too and smiled. They gestured toward the door, so I started moving. Kamenev climbed down the stairs behind me to the tarmac and the waiting car.

"Walt, this is as far as I go." He held out a hand, and we shook. His free hand clasped my forearm. It was a very warm gesture. Nobody had ever shaken my hand like that before.

His eyes were misty as he spoke. "Thank you for the peace you have brought to my Elena. I will sleep so much better now."

There was a lump in my throat, too. "Mr. Kamenev, I can't help but feel like you did a lot more for me than I did for you. I think you saved my life."

The Russian put his hand on my shoulder as he continued to shake my hand. "I saved a life. You will save all of us. Farewell, young man. I hope we meet again."

"We will. I know it."

He turned me to face three people approaching from the car. Two were squat, muscular Japanese men wearing sunglasses and dark suits with no ties. They were flanking a very slight Japanese woman in glasses, her hands clasped behind her back. She looked at Kamenev and gave a slight nod. He returned it, gave me my bag, and started walking back to the jet.

I looked at the woman in front of me, and she was looking me up and down, too. I decided to make an effort to be polite and bowed deep and slow.

She returned the courtesy, as did her bodyguards. A smile tugged at the corners of her prim mouth. I think she liked that. I had so much to learn about this country and a culture that was so much older than my own. It was exciting and terrifying at the same time.

"Walt, I am Dr. Kimiko," she said. "You are to come with us to our facility where we can study you."

"So I'm a lab rat now?"

Her smile grew a little wider. "No, you are a valued resource. Your survival is important."

I suddenly felt very sorry for any lab rats she might own.

"Please enter the car, and our journey will begin." She gracefully gestured toward the limousine. One of the men reached for my bag. I saw some colorful tattoos on his wrist as his sleeve crept up. I handed the bag over immediately. This guy was Yakuza!

The burly guard noticed my surprise and smiled. He knew that I knew. The other guy, probably Yakuza, too, opened the door for the doctor and me.

It was a luxurious ride. There was a full bar, and soft music was playing in the dark interior. There were blue mood lights throughout the long car. The doctor moved right beside me and started digging in a black leather bag. "Please roll up your sleeve. I need blood samples, and I have many questions."

I laughed as I undid a button on my cuff and started rolling up the sleeve of my black dress shirt. "Wow! You don't waste any time."

She didn't look at me as she readied a needle. "That is because there is no time to waste."

# CHAPTER 7

The limousine glided through the streets. Buildings, people, and cars became less and less common as we drove into the country. It was beautiful and peaceful outside, but it was difficult to focus when the good doctor was peppering me with questions.

"How old are you?" she asked as she drew blood.

"Eighteen."

She snapped a test tube out of the needle and put another one in to fill with more of my dark red blood. "How tall are you?"

"Uh…about six feet tall."

The doctor moved her dark almond eyes to look into mine. "Not 'about.' I need an exact height. The last measured."

"Okay, I'm five feet and eleven and a half inches. Exact enough?"

She snapped yet another test tube into place. I

was getting a little weak. "Weight?" she demanded.

"Last I looked, one hundred and eighty-five pounds."

She took the full test tube out and removed the needle. My hands felt weak, and I was relieved to see she was done harvesting. I'd never had so much blood removed at one time.

Dr. Kimiko grabbed a clipboard and wrote for a moment. Probably the answers I'd already given. She was still writing as she asked her next question. "Have you ever had sex?"

I felt my face get hot and flush. "Uh...no."

She gave me a sideways glance, and I thought I detected a slight smirk in the corner of her mouth. "Never?"

"Look, I've messed around, just never...you know. Can you please ask something else?"

She went back to writing. Thank God. "Your surname sounds Russian. Is your heritage, in fact, from that region?"

"I don't know."

Dr. Kimiko gave me a hard look. "You don't know if you're Russian or if there are any other elements in your heritage? Which is it?"

"Uh, both. I'm adopted."

She frowned and wrote on the clipboard. "That is unfortunate."

That was too much. "Listen, it wasn't unfortunate for me! My parents have been amazing.

They couldn't have children, and I didn't have anyone at all. So excuse me for not knowing or caring where I came from."

The doctor gave me a withering look and put down her pen, resting both her hands on the clipboard. "It is unfortunate because we want to run a full genealogy on you and your family. It just got harder. Nothing else was meant."

I was glaring at her, but I realized she was just trying to learn as much as she could. She was doing her job. "Sorry, I'm a little salty. I've been attacked, arrested, chained to a chair, plunked on a plane, and I think you drained me nearly dry. Is it normal to take that much blood?"

She shook her head, and her soft, long hair moved with the motion. "No. I did take more than usual, as we will be forwarding it to labs in this country and others. We must understand what is happening."

"Well, I'm feeling pretty lousy, and my head is spinning." The car took a hard turn on the country roads, and I felt my stomach lurch. "Ohhhh, I'm going to be sick. Pull over!"

She looked over her shoulder and said something in Japanese to the driver. His response was sharp, and he didn't sound pleased, but he pulled over.

I grabbed the door handle and barely got out before I threw up. Oh, *great*. I just met this beautiful Japanese woman, told her I was a virgin, and now I was heaving up my guts on the side of the road. How could she not be charmed?

I could hear the doctor arguing with the driver as they both sat in the car. The other bodyguard had gotten out and was watching me dry-heave. I stole a look his way and gave him a thumbs-up. He just looked away with no expression.

There was the high-pitched sound of a motorcycle coming closer. My stomach was feeling better. At the very least, I was done puking. I stood up straight just in time to see the bike go sailing by me and crash into the ditch beside the limousine. The driver was flying through the air, and he tackled the bodyguard who was standing outside of the car.

I couldn't make out the attacker's face, as he was wearing a helmet with a dark shield. His clothes were old jeans, a filthy jacket, and an old pair of sneakers. What I noticed right away were his hands. His fingernails were like claws, and I could hear him growling and hissing as he and the Yakuza soldier fought for position.

The driver got out, drew a gun, and fired a couple of shots at our assailant. I saw red spots bloom on the grimy jacket, but it didn't slow him down at all. The thing leaped off the man he had pinned on the ground and started running toward me. What happened next will stay with me for the rest of my life.

I felt those rough hands clasp around my neck and start to squeeze, and a voice behind the helmet mask screamed. The hands let go quickly, and the thing jumped backwards. I also heard the two bodyguards emptying their guns into the thing. They needn't have bothered. The hands of our attacker were melting, and in just a couple of seconds, both arms ended in stumps. It fell on the ground, still shrieking, and used the stumps at the ends of its arms to push off the helmet. I wish it hadn't.

The hair was black and greasy, and the eyes on this vampire were pure white. Blood poured from its nose, and the screams sounded like his lungs were full of fluid as it gargled and thrashed. The two Yakuza heavies walked right up to it, removing their sunglasses and staring with wide eyes at the thing dissolving and howling at their feet. One pulled out a phone, took a couple of pictures, and then made a call. The other one just stared at me.

Dr. Kimiko slowly stepped out of the car and stared at the vampire as it stopped moving and died. She looked at me, and her mouth hung open a little. She looked back at the mess on the ground and said, "Well, I have learned more than I thought."

# CHAPTER 8

"Well, that was probably the most horrible thing I've ever seen," I muttered to myself as I sat back into the long, black car. I was still sweating from motion sickness, and I was short of breath.

The doctor leaned forward, and her dark almond-shaped eyes looked into mine. "I've seen much worse."

I believed her. "You said you learned more than you thought. What did you mean by that?"

She sat back and used both hands to smooth her long, black hair off her face. "Kamenev reported that your blood was deadly to these creatures. I have no reason to doubt him on this, but I have seen something most unexpected during that attack." She crossed her arms and frowned. "Your very touch was enough to destroy that thing. It makes me uncertain where to begin my research. My original focus was to be your blood and the antigens it carries. I now consider your

DNA to be worth investigating. Most curious."

"Oh, well, I guess it's good to have a few options. Right?" I rubbed the perspiration out of my eyes and blinked. I was feeling dizzy again.

Kimiko picked up on it and started going through her black bag. "This has been a lot for you. Let me help." She took out a needle and a small bottle.

I held up my hands. "No! No, I'll be fine. I just need a little rest. I just need to sit still for a little while."

"Don't be ridiculous," she muttered, still priming the needle. "You've lost a lot of blood and endured an attack by a vampire. You need more than a quiet moment."

I gave up and let her take my arm. I was starting to feel like a pincushion. Looking out the window seemed like a good idea. I grimaced as I felt the needle go in and deliver its medicine. I couldn't take my eyes off the beauty outside. Small mountains with ice and crags on the top decorated the landscape as we wound through them. "How about answering a question for me? Like, where are we and where are we going?"

The doctor didn't look at me as she disposed of the needle and started rifling in the black bag for something else. "We are driving through the Southern Alps of Japan. That is where our facility is located. You will wake there feeling much better."

Did I hear that right? "What do you mean I will wake…" My vision blurred, and that's the last thing I remember.

***

I woke up in a room. A white room. The sheets, walls, and even the floor were white. Light seeped between the white blinds, and that was enough to help me see everything. The room was so clean, sterile, really. Only the large black television screen on one wall was not gleaming white.

I moved back the sheets to see that I wasn't wearing my street clothes; instead, it was a white uniform like an orderly would wear in a hospital. I wasn't comfortable with the thought that someone had undressed me when I was unconscious. Making it worse was the assortment of small bandages on my arms. I'd obviously been needled a few more times. Other places I won't mention felt odd, too.

The door opened, and Dr. Kimiko strode into the room. "Ah, you are awake. Let me check your vitals."

She was wearing a white lab coat and a blue skirt that showed off toned legs. She sat at the end of the bed and took my pulse. She must have noticed me staring at her sensational legs as she smirked, looking at her watch. "You aren't my type, Walt. Sorry."

"What, American?"

She looked me in the eyes and smiled. "Male."

I felt my eyebrows rise. "Oh," I said, trying to hide my disappointment.

"Is that a problem for you?" she asked as she stuck a thermometer in my mouth and waited for the result.

"Does put a damper on any romantic possibilities," I mumbled.

The doctor smiled, took back the thermometer, and inspected it. "All seems fine. You are in good health. Do you feel a little more rested?"

I did. But I didn't want to make it too easy on her. "Not sure I'm okay with you knocking me out... but yeah, I do feel better. Why did you do that?"

Her slight shoulders lifted in a shrug. "I had no confidence you would be able to sleep on your own. You had just been carsick and attacked by a vampire. It is hard to quiet the mind after such things. Rest was needed, and I just made sure you would have it."

Hard to argue with that kind of logic. "Are you done taking blood and...uh...doing other stuff to me? Do you have what you need?"

"For now," she said, patting my leg. "But I do need to arrange a conversation with the key players to let you know what has transpired since your discovery. It is unprecedented." She pulled out a phone and started working the screen with her thumbs. She nodded at something she read and walked over to the large television facing my bed. Grabbing a remote, she turned it and a sound system on. "Have you done this before?"

"What? What are we doing right now?"

She looked over at me and smiled. "Virtual conference. After you speak, wait a moment for the data to be relayed to the other members of the meeting.

The information is going a great distance."

I saw her bend at the waist, retrieve a small camera, and aim it my way. Then she came and attached a lapel microphone to my shirt. Her jasmine scent was distracting, but I tried to focus. Knowing I didn't have a chance with her helped. Well, a little.

The doctor went back to the screen and pressed a different device, and two faces came on the screen. One was very familiar. "Mister Kamenev!"

My Russian savior smirked and gave me a quick salute. "Zdravstvuj, Walt! You look well."

"Thanks to you!" I looked to the face I didn't recognize: an older African-American man with a bald head and greying hair just over his ears. His glasses were thick and looked like they were wearing him. "I don't think we've met. I'm Walt Baranov," I said with a wave.

He sat there blinking at me, and I was wondering if he heard me when I remembered what the doctor had said. I waited, and sure enough, he responded. "Hello, Walt. I'm Agent Travis Foster. I know things have been a little strange for you, but it is imperative that you understand your situation. The world needs your cooperation, and it needs it right now."

Well, that was a little grim. "Okay, Agent Foster, what's my situation? I mean, I'm in Japan, I've met a really amazing doctor, and I've watched three people you say are vampires die." I raised my arms up at my sides and let them fall with frustration. "Any help?"

Again, that interminable wait. Kamenev and Foster both frowned and started talking at the same time. They both laughed, and Foster gestured for Kamenev to proceed. He gave a tight-lipped smile and nodded acknowledgement at his American counterpart. "I am aware of the two who perished in Russia. I was there, for one. Are we to understand you were bitten again in Japan?"

I shook my head. "No, I wasn't bitten this time."

The doctor strode over to my bed and sat beside me to bring herself into the picture. She leaned into me to speak into my lapel microphone. I smelled that delicious scent of hers again. "Doctor Kimiko here, gentlemen. The subject is correct. His car pulled over to allow him to cope with motion sickness, and there was an attack. The subject was seized by the assailant and immediately started demonstrating the same kind of cellular disruption seen in the previous attacks. It originated at the point of contact and rapidly continued until complete destruction of the assailant." The doctor leaned back and away from my microphone. I was staring at the smooth skin on her neck. She stood up, and I could focus again.

After the predictable delay, I saw the two men raise their eyebrows and sit back in their chairs. It was comical how they both did it at the same time. "Bozhe moi," the Russian muttered.

"Yes, my thoughts exactly," Foster agreed. The American tented his long fingers in front of him.

"Walt, there are a few things we have to tell you. Some of it won't be easy to hear. It's not all bad news. We must proceed very carefully. At this point, we know the vampire communities around the world are aware of your discovery."

Kamenev raised a hand. "They are aware that we have found a young American and that he is dangerous to vampires. Nothing more."

Foster nodded. "If the latest attack was carried out without weapons, then that would reinforce the idea that they know you're dangerous. But that is all they know. That clumsy attempt at the side of the road confirms this."

I held up a hand of my own. "Okay, what does all that mean?"

The American agent pursed his lips. "It means that we have to keep you hidden. If we can't do that, we must keep you moving. If you find yourself in a tough spot, try to touch them. They know you are a danger, but they don't know how. They won't be expecting your touch to be lethal. Who would?"

Kamenev nodded. "I am in complete agreement. I believe the facility you are in now offers the best protection. I would ask the good doctor to talk to her superiors and arrange a contingency plan if the medical research base is compromised."

Kimiko moved in front of me and spoke loud enough that my mic would pick it up. "One is already in place, gentlemen."

"Most satisfactory," Kamenev said with a nod.

"Agreed," Foster echoed. "Walt, the best thing for you to do is listen to the doctor and do not leave that facility for any reason. They may know you're in there, but getting past our Japanese ally's considerable security is another matter entirely. Do you understand?"

I didn't like the sound of that. "So I'm a prisoner here?"

Kamenev shook his head. "You are not a prisoner in a cell, Walt. You are weathering a storm in a castle. There is a difference."

"What do they even do in this place?"

Foster pointed at the doctor. "I believe your host is the best one to answer that question. We'll leave you in her capable hands and meet again if there are any significant developments of any kind. Agreed?"

"Okay, sure," I said with a sigh. What else could I do?

The screen went blank. The doctor's low heels tapped on the tiles as she moved to the large television and turned off the equipment. She turned to me, and that sly half-smile was on her face. "Well, Walt...shall I take you on a tour of the facility? Would you like to see what we do here?"

I gave her a withering look. "My schedule looks pretty clear." I swung my legs out of bed, stood up, and stretched. "Lead on, Doctor."

# CHAPTER 9

We walked down the hall of white tiles and white walls. My slip-on sneakers didn't make a sound, but the doctor's shoes rapped on the finish of the shiny floors. There wasn't a spot of dust anywhere. Did they clean this place ten times a day?

"This is a secret facility, not in its existence, but in its purpose," the doctor explained. "The world's leading scientists and medical professionals live and work here with one purpose in mind."

"Vampires," I guessed.

"Yes, the creatures dubbed 'vampires' by those who encounter them," Kimiko confirmed. "I call them parasites. To me, they are no different than leeches or ticks. Only their size and cunning make them an issue that needs addressing."

She stopped talking when our two Yakuza bodyguards fell in step behind us. I gave them a weak smile and a nod. The two men did little to acknowledge my greeting, but I thought I detected a slight nod. What did I really expect? The Yakuza are not really known for their soft, fuzzy side.

The doctor wasn't kidding about involvement from the rest of the world. You'd think that a secret facility in Japan would have personnel that were predominantly Japanese. You would be wrong. I saw men and women of every race and nationality pass us by.

It was always the same. They would nod reverently at Dr. Kimiko and steal a quick glance at me, almost as an afterthought. I could feel them stop and stare at my back as we walked away. There was reverence for the Doctor and curiosity for me. How much did they really know?

I also picked up on the fact that I was wearing the same clothes that they were. The only thing missing was a lab coat. It was a smart move. Anyone who broke in looking for me would have a tough time. I must have passed ten people who were similar in age and race, and we were all dressed the same. Hard to find one sheep in a herd.

The facility had one enormous floor at ground level and four sublevels that you accessed by escalator. We got to a glass escalator and started to descend. The doctor turned to look at me with that half smile as she continued the tour. "The second sublevel is where I spent most of my time before my promotion to project director."

"Cool! What was it you used to do down here?"

She looked forward and still wore the smile. "I was a hematologist of some note, a blood expert. Ambitious, I threw myself into my work. It was ultimately my discovery of how the virus alters the very DNA of the victim that fast-tracked me to my position."

"That's a huge discovery. I can't imagine being in charge of something so big. I gotta say, I'm impressed!" It had the virtue of being the truth.

The smile slowly left her face. "Science and research were always easier for me than social interactions. It was the only time I felt confident and in control. My peers didn't understand any better than my parents."

We got off the escalator, and she touched my arm to turn me down a long hallway. "I understand," I said after some thought. "I love reading about history, or even reading in general. Being around people for too long stresses me out. Maybe that's why I like being around you. You're not putting on a show, and you know who you are."

She stole a quick glance at me and then turned and pointed to researchers working in a lab behind a huge window. "This entire lab and everyone who works on this floor is dedicated to studying and understanding how this unique virus is transmitted, and they're looking for a way to create antibodies to prevent the emergence of new creatures."

"Oh? How's that going?"

She frowned, still staring into the lab. "Not as well as hoped, I'm afraid. Finding the mechanism that allows the virus to alter the very DNA of the victim should have helped us to find a way to prevent such a change from happening. To date, it has not revealed itself."

We finished walking down the long hall, made it to another escalator, and started descending to the third sublevel. Still, people were walking by and occasionally buzzing by on a white golf cart, always showing respect to Kimiko and doing a double take as I went by. I felt like the new kid in high school.

"This level has a different purpose," the doctor continued, pointing at the teams working in the labs behind the large windows. "All of those on the third sublevel are engineering ways to destroy the creatures that have been infected. It has had even less success than the second level." She looked at me and stopped walking, and I saw a gleam in her eye. "Until you were discovered."

"You're hoping to find something in my blood or DNA to help them, right?"

She looked at me, searching my face. Did I say something wrong? A light chuckle escaped the stoic doctor. "While more research is ongoing, the focus has changed. We no longer seek that which harms them, but why your essence is so destructive. We seek to understand and replicate it."

Did I hear that right? "You want to weaponize it?"

"We do."

I crossed my arms and looked at the floor. I wasn't sure what to say. I wasn't sure what could be said. It all seemed like a runaway train, out of my control. I noticed another escalator at the end of the hall. "What's on the next level?"

The doctor looked over at the escalator and turned back quickly. She took me by the arm and turned me away. "A sublevel. Nothing of any importance. You must be hungry. Allow me to take you to our cafeteria. The food is quite excellent."

Gently taking the doctor's hand off my arm, I looked at her. "Doctor, what's on the fourth sublevel?"

An awkward moment passed. The lovely doctor and I locked eyes, and I could feel her hesitation. Still, she blinked first. "Test subjects," she answered.

"Vampires...you have vampires down there?"

It was her turn to fold her arms over her chest. "Parasites that used to be human. What you call 'vampires.' They live in the fourth sublevel for research purposes. How could we proceed if we did not have access to the virus?"

"I want to see it."

She held up a hand. "I don't think that is necessary."

"What? You said you were going to explain how this facility works. I know this is old news to you, but I've only seen three vampires. I got to watch them die, and that's it."

"Walt..."

"Listen," I interrupted. "If you were me, would you be satisfied with that answer? You wouldn't want to know everything?" I put my hand on her arm, and one of the Yakuza bodyguards gently removed it. Message received.

The doctor said something quickly to the bodyguard and turned her attention to me. "I understand your curiosity, Walt. I just don't see any benefit, and it might be detrimental to your state of mind."

"Doctor, don't you think I've earned the right to know? With everything I've seen and everything I've gone through, you think this is too much?"

She drew a breath and let it out slowly, watching me as she considered my point. I was about to ask again when she slowly nodded. "Okay, Walt. It's time you learned what we're up against. For better or for worse, it's time you knew it all."

# CHAPTER 10

Neither of us said a word as we descended the escalator to the fourth level. It was awkward, the silence and standing so close to each other. She didn't think the test subjects mattered, and I just couldn't see it that way. Our two silent bodyguards were right behind us like dangerous shadows. So why didn't I feel safe?

The differences in the fourth level from the others were subtle but many. The light was a little lower, and while it was just as clean, there was an antiseptic odor in the air. Instead of wide halls and big windows revealing lab workers bustling like busy members of a beehive, there were smaller windows that allowed people in the hall to look into darkened rooms. Every small room had a door with a number on it. Occasionally, there was a name scribbled in marker on tape that had been applied above the digits on the doors.

I walked up to the first cell and looked in. I saw

a fat man with a grey beard curled up in the corner, wearing nothing but a hospital gown. He was just beside the toilet. I saw his dark eyes look toward me, and he lifted a hand as if in greeting. "*Señor, por favor... ayudame!*" his tired voice called to me. I looked above the door and saw a small speaker, obviously meant to facilitate conversation. "*Estoy enfermo...ayudame.*" His voice trailed off weakly as he slumped in the corner.

The doctor came and stood beside me. "You are looking at Pablo. He was captured in Spain about two years ago."

I did a double-take. "You know his name?"

"Oh, yes. I know the history of that test subject," she answered with a smirk. "At least what he did to get himself here."

"He seems pretty harmless. A little pathetic, really."

I felt the doctor's hand turn me to face her. "He had just killed a family of five who felt the same way and offered him shelter when he was captured."

There was a loud slam as the old guy suddenly stood up against the glass, hissing and snarling. His black eyes were malevolent and changed into a glowing green. The teeth in his mouth looked sharp as drool spilled out of the corners of his mouth. Gone was the pathetic old man who needed assistance. In his place stood a heavy monster who radiated hatred. I took a step back. I couldn't help it.

"Have you seen enough?" the doctor asked and

stole a quick look at the elegant, slim watch on her equally delicate wrist.

"No, not yet," I answered. "How many are down here?"

"There are twenty remaining."

"I want to see them all."

That was the limit of the doctor's patience. She turned and said something to one of the bodyguards and turned back to me. "I have better things to do than watch you gawk at monsters. Harada will accompany you while you are here and take you back to your room when you are finished." Without another word, she strode away from me, leaving me with nobody but the impassive Harada.

I let out a sigh and shrugged. Harada just stared at me. "Well, let's meet some more monsters," I muttered and walked to the next cell. This one had a maintenance worker cleaning up. I saw a blackened skeleton on the tiled floor, and the masked worker was mopping up the gore. I'd seen that before. I had to wonder if some of my blood had been used to destroy the occupant of the room. It made me feel ill.

The next few cells held old men and women wearing the same hospital gowns as the first prisoner. They either ignored me or gave me a dirty look and then ignored me. It was sad to see the hopelessness and anger in them. Also, it was a bit disturbing to know that they would rip us limb from limb if they got out. I hadn't forgotten the way the old Spaniard had hit the glass.

I stopped when I came to the last cell. It was a young woman. I could only tell by her feet and hands. She was seated on the floor wearing nothing but a hospital gown and curled in a ball, her arms hugging her legs. Her long, lank, dark hair fell over her face. I found myself staring. She wasn't as old as the others when she became infected. I wondered how long it had been since she had been bitten.

I decided to ask. I tapped on the glass and got no reaction. I saw a red button for an intercom and pressed it. "Uh, hello?" I called out, hoping that the speaker was on and she would hear me. It seemed to work as her face tilted up slowly, and I couldn't believe what I was seeing.

Not only was she very young, but she was so delicate. I pressed the button again. "What is your name?!" I called to her. That seemed to wake something within her as she slowly stood up and crept toward the window. She looked to be about eighteen when she was infected. She staggered forward slowly, and her face pressed against the glass. I heard a high-pitched hiss coming from the speaker as she glared at me.

A bell sounded, and she jumped back from the window of the cell, looking up. An intravenous bag full of blood fell from an opening in the roof, and she leapt on it, breaking the bag with her teeth and gorging herself on the contents. I looked around and saw the other prisoners were doing the same. This must have been a scheduled feeding time.

I was startled when I turned back, and the young woman's face was right there against the glass, her arms high on the window. Her mouth was smeared with blood, and her black eyes looked right into mine. I heard her hiss change and form a whispered word. "*Irina!*" came from the speaker above.

I turned quickly to my bodyguard. "Harada san, please take me back to my room."

# CHAPTER 11

It was a long walk, and I had a lot to think about. I thanked Harada when he opened my door and let me in. He gave his usual nod, and I was alone with my thoughts. They weren't good company.

I sat on the edge of my bed and stared at the floor. I wasn't stressed, just overwhelmed with it all. There was nothing special about me, and nothing profound or miraculous had happened to bring about this strange situation. Yet I'd seen my blood and even my touch turn frightening monsters into pudding. There was no explanation for it, and I started to wonder if they'd ever figure it out.

Really, there was only one thing bothering me, and it was the one thing I couldn't live with. Because of me, people were going to die. Maybe a lot of people. Oh sure, they were dangerous and scary, but they were still people.

The doctor saw them as "subjects" or

"creatures." Not me. I saw people who once had loved ones. I saw fathers and mothers and that poor Irina was somebody's daughter. I couldn't get her out of my mind. She answered my question! It wasn't easy for her, but she *did* answer me. How much of her remained? Did anyone know? Did anyone care?

There was a sharp rap on the door, and Doctor Kimiko walked into the room. "You must be hungry. Will you let me buy you some lunch?"

I just couldn't stay mad at her. "Yeah, lunch sounds good." I stood up. "Are we talking take-out or delivery?"

Her eyes softened. "Neither. A sit-down meal, and I think you will find it is excellent quality."

"Are you joining me?"

"Yes, I will join you."

I clapped my hands together and gave her a grin. "Lady, you've got yourself a date."

Her smirk reappeared. "It is most certainly not a date, Mister Baranov."

"Two people eating a meal together, and I think you did the asking." I shrugged. "Sounds like a date to me."

She laughed and turned her back on me as she left the room. "I think your ears hear what they want, Walt. This has been explained to you already."

Yeah, I had no chance. But it was still fun to joke about it. Probably the only amusement I was likely to have around this place.

I hustled to catch up to her. I found the doctor marched more than walked when she had somewhere to go. An overachiever in all ways, but she was the only one I knew in this world of science and research. "So where are we going?"

She didn't look at me as she answered. "This facility is equipped with an excellent food service area. Prepare to be impressed."

"Japanese food? I'd like to try some while I'm in Japan."

"Of course."

"Sushi?"

"Fresh and delicious," she answered, trying to suppress a smile.

I put my hands in my pockets as we walked. "I'm going to need some help with a couple of things."

"Like what?"

"How to use the chopsticks...and what food there actually counts as sushi."

She stopped and gave me a look. "You've never tried it? Never?"

"We're still talking about sushi, right?"

She brought a hand to her mouth and could not stop the laugh that escaped and echoed down the hall. A few people walking by stared at us as they passed. She gave me a playful swat. "Come on, Walt. Let's get you some experience."

# CHAPTER 12

"I can see why this is a big deal," I mumbled with a mouth full of tuna roll. "It's a nice flavor, especially with the wasabi and soy sauce."

The doctor finished what she was eating and shook her head. "I think you drowned that delicacy in sauce and spice. Still, we have excellent sushi chefs. Some of the best."

Looking around, I had to marvel at the size of the place. When we'd walked in, I thought it was just another cafeteria. Then I noticed the little things. The place was clean. I mean, it was the cleanest! The chairs were not the crappy steel and plastic you would expect. No, they were a very comfortable bamboo and leather, like something you would see in someone's home.

What surprised me most was the selection in the serving area. I wanted the sushi, for sure, but I had many other choices. American, Italian, and I think there were even some African dishes. That I did not expect.

Attention was the other part of our dinner that I didn't anticipate. I could feel the eyes of everyone staring at me as we ate. Even the ones not staring were looking out of the corners of their eyes. Were stories circulating? Or were they figuring out that I was the source of the blood that was lethal to their "test subjects?"

I stabbed another tuna roll with a chopstick, dipped it in soy, and jammed it in my mouth as my dinner partner winced at the improper use of the traditional Japanese eating utensils. After swallowing it down, I used the other chopstick to point around the room. "Hey, Doctor...all these people pretending not to stare at me. They're from all over the place, aren't they?"

Kimiko took the cloth napkin and dabbed at her mouth. "Yes, they're experts from all over the world. Some have been here for years." She took the chopstick from me. "Please don't do that. It's considered impolite."

"And the staring? That's polite?"

She looked around, and people who were watching snapped their heads back into conversations or the meal in front of them. The doctor looked at me with a smile. "You must forgive them. They have been working for so long to make the smallest of steps in understanding the vampire phenomenon. Word has traveled, and they are all being provided with blood samples that have extraordinary properties. They know something big is happening, and they have doubtlessly reasoned that you are the source of this blood. You cannot blame them for being excited."

Made sense to me. "Okay, I get it. Feels a bit weird, but I get it." I grabbed my cloth napkin and cleaned my own mouth. "Listen, since I'm going to be here for a little while, can I do some research of my own?"

The doctor frowned. "You were training as an anthropologist in college before your father was assigned to Russia, were you not?"

"Yes, I was. Studying different cultures and societies is what I like to do. I'm interested in learning more about vampires' behavior. Who do they become once they're infected?"

Kimiko sat back in her chair and shook her head. "I was afraid of this. Your time on the fourth level has clearly affected you."

"I wouldn't say that. I'd call it a bit of a breakthrough. I'm not asking for anything that costs money or risks my neck or anyone else's."

She arched an eyebrow. "Then what are you asking for, exactly?"

I rubbed my hands together, thinking how to ask. "Well, I just want to talk to them. Actually, just one of them."

Her eyes stayed locked on mine. "Which subject did you seek to interview?"

"Number twenty, her name is Irina."

Both the doctor's hands came down on the table hard, slapping the smooth surface. She sat there, blinking at me. "How did you learn her name?"

I shrugged. "I asked, and she told me."

Kimiko leaned very close to me. "She actually told you?" she whispered.

"Yes! It wasn't easy for her. With your permission, I'd like to go to the fourth sublevel at a very specific time and just keep asking her questions. I promise to write down anything she says and report to you. Would that be okay?"

The doctor took a sip of her water and mulled it over. "I'll allow it, but you must be accompanied by Harada when you go. That's the only way it will be permitted. Do you understand?"

"Sure, sure! I kinda like the tough guy. What are the Yakuza doing involved in this, anyway?"

My dinner companion shook her head. "They're here to help accomplish what every single person in this facility desires."

"Which is what?"

"The complete and utter eradication of vampires from the world."

# CHAPTER 13

Wasn't glad to be back in my bed, but the doctor had to do her job, and now I was getting more and more tired. She snapped another test tube into the spigot, and I watched still more blood leave my body. I was getting light-headed.

The lovely doctor stifled a yawn, and it hit me that I wasn't the only one feeling the fast pace of this research. "You look tired too, Doc. Are you getting any sleep?"

She gave a slight shrug. "I am, but even when I am resting, my mind is not at peace. You have presented an interesting and fascinating puzzle, Walt. It is not one that I can leave behind, and it always occupies my thoughts."

"Are you...are you kind of enjoying this?"

"I am." She patted my arm after taking out the full test tube and snapping in another one. "Discovering the mysteries in your blood will complete work that I have dedicated my life to solving."

"You're taking a lot of blood," I pointed out. "I think I heard you say something about synthesizing it? Have you done that yet?"

She shook her head, her long, straight hair moving slightly on her shoulders with the motion. "No. I need more blood to send to laboratories around the world. We have not succeeded in synthesizing anything yet. You will know the minute we accomplish this feat."

"You'll tell me?"

"No." The doctor removed the last tube and the needle that was supplying the tubes. "You will find yourself on a plane back to Russia or the United States. You will be free." She put a bandage on my arm.

"Will you come and say goodbye before I go?"

Her eyes looked into mine, and she smiled. One hand touched my face tenderly. "Of course. I will never forget meeting you. I have come to enjoy our conversations." She grabbed her bag and headed toward the door. "I've drawn a lot of blood. You need rest, Walt. When you wake, I will arrange another conference to discuss my findings and find out what our people on the outside have learned."

I hated to admit it, but rest seemed like a great idea. I yawned and waved weakly as the doctor left my room. Sleep came fast.

\*\*\*

When my eyes opened later, I was alone. I got up

and still felt a little woozy. Steadying myself, I used the bathroom attached to my room and looked in the mirror. I looked at the guy staring back and took stock. All the sleep meant no circles under my eyes, but was I ever pale. I wondered if there was something I should be eating to help my body produce more red blood cells. I made a note to ask the doctor. She'd know.

Doctor Kimiko. So conflicted when it came to her. I mean, I found her incredibly hot but kind of cold at the same time. Not her sexual orientation, of course. We are who we are. No, it was the way she thought nothing of the "test subjects." How could she be so callous? I was pretty sure she wouldn't give me the time of day if it wasn't for my magical blood. Would she?

Harada came through the door, followed by the doctor. The Japanese heavy and I exchanged a nod, and the doctor gave me her usual small smile. Very professional. "Glad you're awake. Are you able to partake in the conference?"

"Sure." I slid back into bed. "Still a little light-headed. Can I lie down for the meeting?"

"Of course," she answered as she fired up the television and readied the camera. She approached the bed, the lapel microphone in her hand. She sat on the bed beside me, and I got to enjoy the closeness and her presence. Part of me enjoyed that, and part of me felt like an idiot. I did notice she was very good with her hands, and she handled attaching the microphone easily.

Kimiko said something to Harada, and he walked over to the television, turned it on, and walked back with a lapel mic for the doctor as well. That made sense. The first conference was to bring me up to speed. This one promised to involve everyone.

The screen gave a flicker, then split into two frames, and the two faces I expected were looking at us. "Hello to our friends in Japan," Agent Foster announced.

"Hello, Walt, Doctor Kimiko," Kamenev echoed.

"Greetings, gentlemen," the doctor called.

I just waved a hand at them. Didn't feel terribly talkative. I still felt a little weak, and I was hoping they wouldn't pick up on it. I was hoping for too much.

Kamenev frowned. "Walt, are you well? You do not look yourself."

I couldn't help liking the older Russian. "I'm okay, Comrade! Just getting a little low on blood. I'll make some more. It's pretty popular with the scientists around here."

The two men on the screen gave a small laugh. The doctor clasped her hands behind her back and lifted an eyebrow at me as if to say, *really*?

"Can you provide us an update on your research, Doctor?" Foster asked. Kamenev nodded his agreement when the question reached him in Russia.

Doctor Kimiko easily walked on her heels to retrieve a clipboard and addressed the two men on the screen. "Our research is nowhere near complete, but the findings thus far have been extraordinary."

I was starting to see why she was so tired. The entire time she was playing hostess to me, her team was working hard, and she was overseeing the entire operation. No easy feat.

She found what she was looking for and continued. "We have a greater understanding regarding the mechanism that makes Mister Baranov's blood so destructive to the creatures we have been studying. There are two elements to this rather violent chemical reaction."

"It's a chemical reaction? It happens very fast," said Kamenev.

"Yes. Walt has antigens in his blood that actively destroy the virus that inhabits and dominates these so-called vampires."

"That explains the blood, but it doesn't explain the fact that his touch is also deadly to these things," Agent Foster pointed out.

The doctor smiled and looked down at her notes. "That's the part that is the most fascinating and may ultimately help us understand how this phenomenon exists at all."

"Please, go on." Kamenev leaned forward in his seat as he pressed her.

"We know the virus rewrites the DNA of the victim. It takes twelve hours to fully take hold, and the change is profound. Anyone infected loses the ability to manufacture their own red blood cells, making them dependent on acquiring what they need from their victims. This never-ending thirst makes them irrational and aggressive. There have been reports that those infected are faster and stronger than average, and this has been proven. We believe it to be only a slight increase. Their senses do become much sharper, and it is probably an adaptation to help them hunt and evade detection."

Foster raised a hand to get her attention. "Is this the reason that they don't age? This rewriting of the DNA?"

She nodded her agreement. "Yes. This is something that has been studied in the scientific community for years. We have harvested cancerous cells that do not age and have had success slowing the cell activity using four genes in mice. These vampires can be incredibly old because their DNA has been rewritten, stunting the aging process."

I wasn't following. "Okay, but this doesn't explain why my touch makes everything …uh…fall apart on these things."

The doctor smiled at me. "You are closer than you know. Your DNA reacts to the DNA of the infected in a rather surprising way. The substances in your cells will not tolerate the rewriting that has occurred in the cells of the victims of this infection. If they touch, the DNA in their cells completely gives up the alteration done by the virus. The cells just let go of essential elements of their DNA sequence."

There was silence after this information. I couldn't believe what I was hearing. "So their cells just kind of collapse?"

She pointed at me. "Yes, once a cell lets go of its essential components, any cell it was touching does the same. The creatures fall apart as each cell in their body falls apart, one at a time."

"Like a house of cards," Kamenev mused.

The doctor pointed at him. "Ah, yes! Very much like a house made of cards."

Foster spread his hands in surrender. "All quite fascinating, but I'm still wondering why young Walt there has this quality in his very genetic makeup. Why him?"

Doctor Kimiko set down the clipboard and brought a hand to her chin. "We have a couple of working theories, but we have not been able to verify them. We put a team of researchers on the task of finding the lineage of Walt Baranov. They were unable to track down the identity of his parents, but the circumstances of his birth are very interesting."

I couldn't believe what I was hearing. Nobody could find out who my parents were? I mean, nothing? You'd think there would be something. Some trace record of who they were and some clue as to why I was surrendered.

The doctor stole a quick glance at me and continued. "Baranov was actually born in Croatia. He was abandoned on the stairs of a church and forwarded to an orphanage in Russia. This makes no sense. What was the need to move him from Croatia?"

Foster nodded. "Someone wanted that baby in another country for a reason, even if we can't know what it was."

She pursed her lips and continued. "I find it interesting that the first recorded incidence of vampirism was in Croatia, and that's also where our young friend came into the world. There is the possibility that the population was eventually able to build a natural resistance to the virus. It is something we've seen before."

Kamenev shook his head. "A plausible explanation, but it does not address the fact that nobody else from Croatia, or anyone else in the world, has demonstrated this resistance."

Foster shrugged. "Maybe we just haven't found others yet. There may be people out there who just haven't been bitten by a vampire."

"You are both right," the doctor announced. "The theory is not without flaws, but it's plausible."

"What is the other theory you are considering?" Kamenev pressed. "You said there was more than one."

The doctor took a breath and stole a quick glance at me before letting it out. She was preparing herself for something. But what?

"When a baby is born to an HIV-positive mother,

sometimes it has the virus, and sometimes it does not. If antiretroviral treatment occurs, it becomes more likely the baby will be clear of infection at birth. Some time ago, a story circulated of a baby whose mother was HIV positive, and the baby was able to defeat the virus on its own."

"The 'Mississippi Baby.' I remember reading about this," Foster added.

"Yes, but this was later proven to be false," the doctor continued. "However, the levels of the virus were greatly reduced, which was certainly promising."

There was a lingering silence as we digested where she was going. Kamenev was the first to speak up. "You believe our friend is descended from a vampire?"

"We believe his mother was a vampire at the time of his birth, yes." The doctor looked back at me. "I am sorry to tell you this, Walt."

"There's no way!" I objected. "I mean...you've seen the things. What vampire is going to get, uh, get romantic with anyone when they're like that? All they want to do is kill and feed."

"I admit, it seems unlikely, but there's still so much we don't know about this virus. These creatures still have the necessary organs and gametes necessary to produce a child. Perhaps the virus had not completely taken hold when you were conceived. We will never know."

I couldn't believe what she was saying.

Sometimes I wondered about my biological parents but never had a need to find out. I figured that they were in a spot and wanted me to have a better chance. Or they were addicts. My mother was a vampire? I must confess that I never, ever entertained that fantasy.

The doctor had silently moved beside me and placed a delicate hand on my shoulder. "It does explain why you were moved so quickly out of the country. They were afraid."

"Afraid of the monster baby?" I said, still looking down.

"No," she corrected gently. "I believe you were abandoned to spare you from certain death, and those at the church wanted you as far away from harm as possible. Either she died in childbirth, or your mother conquered that unbearable thirst to save you. We can never know how hard that must have been. You must remember that, Walt."

Foster shook his head. "Extraordinary. But there's no way to confirm this theory, am I right?"

Kamenev shook his head. "Actually, the doctor's theory may be confirmed by the most unlikely of sources. The vampires themselves."

"Please explain," the doctor said, walking back towards the screen.

The Russian cleared his throat. "We have been closely monitoring the Internet and pushing our sources for more information. There was a meeting of all the most important vampires in Rome a couple of days ago."

"Rome? Really?" I interrupted. "At the Coliseum or something?"

"The Vatican, actually," Kamenev explained.

Foster bristled. "You can't believe the Catholic Church is involved in this, Ivan."

"No," said his counterpart. "There are those in the Catholic organization that arranged a hidden, secret, and safe meeting place. An emergency meeting, I should add."

"Did anything come out of the meeting that would confirm or refute our theory?" asked the doctor.

"Possibly." Kamenev rubbed his hands together and gathered his thoughts. "They are afraid. They know of Walt and the significance of his discovery. There was also talk of a prophecy, and it was brought up more than once. In Russian, they are calling Walt, '*Syn Meduzy.*'"

"What? What does that even mean?" I asked.

"Loosely translated, it is a prophecy about the son of a monster that will bring the whole vampire nation down. *Syn Meduzy* means 'Medusa's Son.' A vampire legend that is about eighteen years old. It started about the time of your birth."

All eyes turned to me. I just stared at my lap. "If it's all the same to you, I think I'd like to be alone right now."

# CHAPTER 14

I don't remember much of what happened next. I think the two men on the screen said goodbye or something encouraging. I didn't care. How could I?

I do remember the doctor coming to me and speaking quietly. "Walt. I am worried about your color. I want you to eat some dinner. A steak, if you will."

"I don't really feel like leaving my room, Doctor."

She rubbed my arm. "I understand. I will have Harada bring it to you. Will you please eat it?"

I shrugged. "Sure. You're the doctor, right?"

When she didn't answer, I looked up. I wasn't sure what I saw in her eyes. She ruffled my hair and smiled. "Thank you."

They both walked out and left me in that silent, white room. I was probably the son of a monster. My birth, my existence, was a sign to a nation of horrible creatures that their death was imminent. For vampires,

I was the devil, or no…the Antichrist that would bring about the end of their world.

I really missed being a student whose father worked at the American Embassy in Russia. I spent years cultivating that life, that identity. I wanted it back. I was never one who craved the spotlight. I didn't want to be important. I didn't want everyone to know who I was.

What if I'd never gone to the Dancing Duck that night? I'd lived my whole life without being bitten by a vampire. I'll bet I could have made it another eighteen years without getting chomped. Maybe more.

True to the doctor's word, Harada arrived with a nice steak dinner on a tray. A tall glass of water was included to wash it down. It made sense. Red meat for the benefits to the circulatory system and water to keep me hydrated.

While part of me wished the doctor was still around because I never tired of hearing her talk, part of me was also glad I didn't see her. I couldn't get her "theories" out of my head. I know she was just doing her job, but I needed a little time to process.

The more I thought about it, the more I realized there was only one person I wanted to see. I polished off my steak and carried the tray to the door. I was looking for Harada. Luckily, he and Ito were standing guard outside my room.

***

The fourth sublevel was creepy. I don't know if it was

because it was dark and deserted or because it smelled so sterile and antiseptic. Might also have been because it was jammed full of vampires who were just itching to feed. That was unique.

I felt all their eyes on me as Harada and I walked the halls. It wasn't hate or malice of any kind that I sensed. It was hunger. They were looking at me like I was their lunch. Even that nasty old schemer Pablo had given up playing possum and paced in his cell. He was truly frightening.

The irony was that I was far more dangerous to them than they were to me. If only they knew. Locked up for study purposes, they probably had no idea of what the rest of their community was discussing. Were they whispering my name to each other out there? Did it strike fear into their hearts? The rumors of 'Medusa's Son' were making the rounds.

I could feel Harada's unease. My silent escort looked around constantly as I made my way through the dreaded fourth level. No researchers here. Nobody stayed here longer than they had to.

When I made it to cell twenty, my heart sank. I couldn't see her anywhere. Had they tested my blood on her? Was she dead?

Then I saw her. It was only the edge of a dirty foot and one toe. She was curled into a ball under her bed. Was she hiding from the light? Was she cold? There was so much I wanted to know, but it would have to wait.

I walked up to the button to communicate. I pressed it and spoke. "Irina? It's me. I'm Walt. I am the person who asked your name yesterday. Do you remember?"

A high-pitched hiss came from beneath the bed. I didn't know what it meant. No way to interpret that.

"Irina, I know talking, even thinking, is probably very hard for you right now. You are going to feed, and then we can talk. Okay?"

Again, that hiss. But it was quieter, not as fierce. A bell rang, and a clear bag filled with blood fell from the ceiling. She scrambled from under the bed and savaged the bag, smearing blood all over her face and hands. Her eyes glowed an ungodly green as she wolfed it down as fast as she could. She let out a long sigh when she had finished and turned to look at me and my escort. Her hospital gown was filthy, and her dark hair hung lank over her face. She slowly stepped toward the glass.

I don't know why, but I put my hand on the glass where she could see it. She did the most curious thing. She reached for it with one of her own and pressed her palm up against the glass, mirroring my hand, and set her head against the pane. Her eyes were dark again, and she stared into mine.

I waved with my other hand, and she mimicked the movement. Did she understand me, or was she just toying with her food? "Hello, Irina. My name is Walt. Do you remember?"

"*Walt*," she hissed eerily. It sounded strange coming through the small speaker on the door. No warmth in her voice at all.

"Yes, I'm Walt. Do you speak English?"

She smiled a little, revealing fangs. "*Small English*," came back from the speaker.

"Good! That's good!" I couldn't believe we were communicating at all. I hesitated, fumbling for my next words. "Do you remember life before...before you were this? Before you were always hungry?"

She looked down and then up into my eyes, into my soul. "*I remember.*"

This was going better than expected. "What do you remember? Do you remember a family? A father? Mother? Do you—"

"*Papa!*" she interrupted. "*Papa! Mama! Ospasnost!*" She started crying, and it was the saddest thing I ever saw. Instead of tears, rivulets of blood oozed down her cheeks. She tried to wipe it away but only succeeded in smearing it on her face.

"Do you remember anything else? Did you have any pets? A dog? A cat?"

"*Sobaka! A dog*," she hissed and put both hands on the glass, looking at me.

"Okay, great! What was the name of the dog? Can you remember, Irina?"

She tilted her head back and looked at me with those haunting eyes. "*Boris. Dog name, Boris.*"

"His name was Boris?"

"*Her name. Boris was girl.*"

I laughed and shook my head. "You named a girl dog Boris?"

"*Was mistake.*" She laughed too and, for the first time, sounded like a young woman.

"Can you remember anything else from before?"

"*Must rest,*" she sighed and looked down at the floor.

"Irina, please. Can you remember anything else?"

"*Rest...must rest.*" She hissed and turned from the glass.

"Okay, okay! Can we talk again, Irina?"

She stopped in her tracks and looked over her shoulder. "*Okay, Walt.*" She didn't say another word, just crawled under her bed and curled up.

It was over. This brief but revealing meeting was done. I looked over at Harada, and I saw something I had never seen from him. His eyes were wide, and he stared into the cell like I wasn't there. He was surprised by all of it. "Harada san, could you please get a blanket and put it in her cell?"

He shook his head and clasped his hands in front of him. "No can do that." His English was reasonable, albeit with a heavy Japanese accent.

I walked up to him and pleaded with him. "Harada san, I can't do it. If there's any of my DNA on the blanket, Irina will die. You know this to be true. I'm only asking you because I can't do it. I take full responsibility."

The tough Yakuza standing in front of me let out a sigh and gave a quick nod. I saw him walk away to get the blanket. I turned back to the cell and lowered myself to see Irina under her bed. "I will be back tomorrow. Okay?" No answer came back.

Harada came back with a small blue blanket. He opened a slot on the side of the cell and fed it in slowly. It landed beside the bed. A small, pale hand filthy with dried blood reached out and slowly drew it underneath the bunk.

I smiled and walked over to Harada. I bent at the waist and gave him a deep bow. "Thank you, Harada san."

He returned my bow and gestured toward the exit.

I laughed. "Yeah, you're right. Definitely, time to go." I'd seen all I needed to see.

# CHAPTER 15

"Walt! I need to speak with you!" called the doctor from down the hallway. I was just coming back from the serving area with a coffee, Harada was beside me.

"Ah! I was hoping to talk with you, too." I responded. A much nicer tone than the one she was using.

I watched the good doctor march toward us, heels rapping on the immaculate white tiles. "Not happy," Harada muttered under his breath.

"Yeah, I got that, too," I whispered back. Then, with a winning smile, I called out, "Hello, Doctor Kimiko! What's on your mind?"

"Am I to understand you placed a blanket for the test subject in cell twenty?" Her eyes didn't blink as she glared at me.

"Yes, her body language told me that she was cold."

"Walt, you know better than anyone what

would happen if any of your DNA were to come in contact with the test subject!"

"Irina," I replied.

"What?"

"Her name is Irina. It's all good, Doctor. I asked Harada to put it in there for me. I take full responsibility, of course."

She stole a quick glance at Harada, who gave a quick nod and turned her attention back to me. "Keeping those cells sanitary is a challenge for the staff who work the fourth level as it is. The creatures have no interest in keeping clean or maintaining their room in any way. That blanket is sure to become caked with dried blood and other filth."

I shrugged. "It's there to keep her warm. She's using it now, isn't she?"

The doctor glared daggers at me and crossed her arms on her chest. "She is."

"Don't worry, Doctor Kimiko," I said and held up a hand. "I won't put anything else in there. No pillows, no bathrobes, no magazines. Okay?"

She pursed her lips and narrowed her eyes at me. "I granted you a favor, allowing you to visit the fourth level. Keep your word, and do not make me regret this decision."

"Aren't you interested to find out what I learned? Since you're trying to learn as much about the virus as you can, aren't you interested to see what remains of the people infected?"

Her eyebrows lifted, and I took that as a sign of curiosity. "Very well. What have you discovered?"

I rubbed my hands together. "That they're still in there! The person they were before they were attacked is there, dormant, just below the surface."

"And you know this, how?"

"Irina knows her name. She remembers her parents and parts of her childhood when asked. She can even see the humor in events that have passed. Tell me, Doctor, have you ever taken the time to speak with them?"

"Walt, nobody at this facility has spent any time socializing with these things for very good reason."

This I didn't expect. "Why not? I mean...they're not going anywhere."

Kimiko took a breath and let it out slowly. "I was hoping you would figure this out for yourself, but you have not." She walked closer to me, looking up into my face. "Walt, every single person in this facility has lost a loved one to these horrible creatures. Every single one."

I just stood there blinking. It hadn't occurred to me at all. I looked over at my escort. "Harada?" I asked.

A nod.

"Have you never wondered why the Yakuza are involved in this research?" the doctor pressed. "Shall I tell you?"

"Yeah, I did wonder about that. Everyone knows

who the Yakuza are, and that they are not to be messed with, but their interests are usually, uh, elsewhere. I also believe there is some serious friction between the Russians and the Yakuza over a land claim. Am I right, Harada?"

"Hai," Harada confirmed.

The doctor put her fingers on my chin and turned my face to look at hers. "Well, what you don't know is that the creatures took the lives of many Yakuza and members of their families in a bloody turf war in Tokyo. They are sworn enemies, and your discovery means that the power struggle is effectively over."

I couldn't believe what I was hearing. "So you're not really interested in helping these people? You just want to wipe them out?"

"Yes, Walt. I am charged with the solemn duty to find a way to eliminate these creatures once and for all time. My mission, my goal, is to destroy every vampire in the world."

I blinked at her. "Have you been given this mission by the Japanese government or the Yakuza?"

"Both. The goal serves the needs of both organizations, and the Russians have been most supportive in this regard. It is the only thing on which both nations agree."

"Okay, I understand." I shrugged. "I get it. Thanks for explaining it to me."

The doctor's face softened. "I am glad we have come to an understanding. I will meet you in your room to draw more blood and check your vitals in an hour." She turned and started walking away.

"Doctor, can you arrange a meeting with the Yakuza? There are things they need to know and things I wish to discuss."

She stopped dead in her tracks and looked at me over her shoulder, eyes wide. "Yes, I believe I can arrange that. I will tell you this, Walt, you may regret this request." She turned and walked away.

# CHAPTER 16

The silence in the limousine hung like an angry cloud between us. True to her word, Kimiko had arranged a meeting and even found a navy suit and tie that fit me well. I guess it wouldn't do to sit down with a bunch of murderous gangsters without dressing up. Still, I had to trust the doctor. It was her show.

I stole a glance at the beautiful doctor, looking out the window. She had really refined her look for what was to come. A matching black skirt and blazer made her silver necklace and matching earrings gleam. Her long dark hair was free, and she had even changed her glasses to wear an elegant, frameless version. My eyes went down to her perfect legs. I noticed she was wearing a little more heel than usual. She was gorgeous.

She turned her head from the window and caught me looking. I quickly turned my gaze to my hands in my lap. I felt my face get hot, which made getting caught even worse.

The doctor just gave me that knowing smile. Ugh! I hated knowing that she knew. "Walt, I must prepare you for this meeting. You must understand how to behave and how to respond. Rudeness will not be tolerated by this organization."

"I have no intention of being rude to the Yakuza. I don't want them to take all my blood at once, thanks!"

She smiled. "You are wise to consider the worst-case scenario. Those who do not are not usually long for this world." She leaned forward in her seat. "There will be one man in the room who is the head of the organization. You may hear others refer to him as 'Oyabun,' which literally translates to 'boss.'"

I wiped my sweating palms on my thighs. "How will I know which one is the boss?"

Again, the smile. "There will be no doubt who leads. You need not concern yourself. Remember that you must always bow first as a sign of respect and hold it until they finish their response. Speak only when spoken to, and do not speak too much."

"Okay, that sounds simple. I can do that."

She smoothed her skirt and looked out the window. She didn't look at me as she spoke. "There is another matter. If you remember, I explained that you were not my type when we met. Do you remember this conversation?"

I shrugged. "Sure. No big deal. What about it?"

"I would appreciate it if you never spoke of it. Certainly not to the Yakuza."

"Uh, okay." I frowned. "I'll respect your wishes, but it's not a big deal. Is it?"

She smiled as she looked out the window. "Homosexuality is viewed as a western problem."

I just blinked at her. "Are you serious?"

"Quite."

"Wow, I thought that sort of thinking was… done."

She looked at me with those dark eyes and a warm smile. "It is a strange situation. Most people in Japan support same-sex marriage, and it is legal to be gay in this country. But still…"

I held up a hand. "It's not talked about, or it is discouraged?"

She nodded and looked out the window. "One politician expressed the belief that we are not productive members of our society because we do not increase the population. I am not ashamed, but I prefer privacy in this matter. Do you understand?"

"Of course! I won't say anything to anyone. I will respect your wishes, but you should be proud of who you are. I think you're amazing."

The doctor turned toward me, and I saw something I hadn't seen before. I couldn't tell if it was gratitude or affection or some mix of both. "Thank you, Walt. That means a lot to me."

Nothing else was said for the rest of the trip. I wasn't sure what had just happened, but I liked it. Now, there was only the meeting with the Yakuza. I felt my hands sweat just thinking about it.

***

The countryside gave way to the urban wonder of Tokyo. The lights, traffic, and sights were like candy for the eyes. I couldn't stop looking out the window. Everything was different. I couldn't believe how many people would cross the street when we were waiting for the lights to change. A sea of humanity would move as one to the other side of the street. Nobody seemed affected, and everyone had somewhere to be. Me too.

We eventually entered a parking garage and kept winding down and down into the depths. Finally, the car was parked, and the door to the limousine was opened by the impassive Harada. The doctor got out first, and I thanked our escort as I exited the car. A short nod was all he gave.

The doctor led the way as we marched through the dark cement world. We were deep in the ground, and the only sound was our shoes on the smooth concrete. An interesting place for a meeting. Secrecy guaranteed, no matter what happened. It wasn't comforting.

We eventually came to a steel door and there were two heavies in black suits on either side. They both had earpieces and were all business as we approached. They looked us up and down and gave a quick nod to our escorts as they opened the heavy steel door. The hinges protested with loud squeaks until the door was completely open.

The doctor didn't hesitate to walk us through the door, and we had to hurry to keep up with her pace. She wasn't nervous, and she had been there before. That much was clear.

It got even darker as we walked, but there were some lights in the distance. There was a crowd of men and women sitting in chairs at the end of the large corridor. One man in the center had a light shining directly on him, and his chair was slightly higher than all the others. His grey hair was slicked back, and his face was impassive. He wore a white suit which seemed to glow under the lightbulb.

The doctor was right. It was not hard to recognize the boss.

# CHAPTER 17

There were no chairs for us, only the inner circle of the Yakuza and the man they called "Oyabun." We just stood in front of them.

When the doctor bowed, so did I, and I held it until the boss gave a short bow and straightened out. The man in charge wore a tight-lipped smile. We were off to a good start. I made a mental note to listen to the doctor on all matters of protocol when it came to the Yakuza. She knew what she was talking about. Why would a hematologist understand the inner workings of the notorious Japanese underworld?

I didn't understand the formalities, as they were all in Japanese, but I could tell this was important to all involved. Everyone in attendance was focused on whoever was speaking, and nobody interrupted. The doctor was doing most of the talking, and the boss would prompt her. At a certain point, his attention turned to Harada.

He asked questions of the foot soldier, who did not hesitate to answer. Harada pointed at me and spoke quickly. The boss looked at Ito and seemed to be asking him for confirmation. Ito nodded without hesitation, and the boss turned my way. He stood up and slowly walked to stand in front of me. Even though I was taller, I felt smaller than the older gangster looking me in the eye. "Is it true?" he asked slowly, with a heavy accent. "You kill vampires. With touch?"

"Yes, Oyabun san. But not by choice."

I heard the doctor sigh beside me. The boss just smiled a little wider. I guess you don't throw the "san" on the end of that sentence.

"We are happy to find you, Walt," the old man announced. "You are the key to destroying our old enemies. The hated Kyūketsuki will know final darkness, and our loved ones will be at peace."

"Ah! On that, I was hoping I could ask for something…uh…different."

I felt the room hold its breath. The Oyabun nodded and went back to his chair. He held up a hand and gestured to me. "We are grateful for your assistance, and Doctor Kimiko says you have been most cooperative. You may ask whatever you wish."

"Thank you, Oyabun." I made sure I didn't throw anything else into the statement. "I know you're going to use my blood, my DNA, to defeat your enemies. I'm okay with that. I am. Part of me even wants them gone. I'd sleep easier knowing they don't exist anymore. But

I'm asking for a different solution."

"Walt, be careful," the doctor cautioned me.

"He may speak. Do not interrupt again, Kimiko!" the Oyabun barked with surprising vigor.

"Yes, my thanks again, Oyabun. I know that the plan is to weaponize what I carry inside. I am asking you to refocus the facility's efforts to find a cure, maybe even a vaccine! You can still get rid of your enemies but save lives as well. I believe this is possible. I believe Doctor Kimiko can achieve this."

There was silence as my request was considered. The length of the silence was getting uncomfortable. Did I cross the line? Finally, the boss nodded slowly. "Why do you ask this?"

"Uh, well…Oyabun, I have spoken to some of those infected at the facility. Some are mindless monsters, but they do have moments of clarity. There are times when they remember what they were and who they are. Details from childhood or a relative from their past. I think…I think that is a sign that they can still be reached. If the thing that has infected them is killed, the virus eliminated, will the person remain? Isn't that a chance worth taking?"

"No," the boss replied. He didn't say another word.

"So that's it?" I asked. "No more discussion?"

"Walt!" Kimiko hissed at me. *"Do not talk anymore!"*

The Oyabun stood up, and so did everyone else

who was seated. What had I done? "You are young, Walt. You are American, so you do not know our ways. I am grateful for what you have done to help our organization and the world. So I will forgive this disrespect."

I held up both hands. "I apologize, Oyabun. I meant no offense. I really didn't!"

The old man walked right up to me and nodded. "I know this. Which is why I can forgive you. I will tell you this, Walt. The hatred between the Yakuza and the Kyūketsuki goes back hundreds of years. These things are not so mindless as you believe. They have targeted the Yakuza and take delight in killing our children. Even after we retaliate, they focus on our people. We have a chance to destroy the hated enemy. There will be no cure. There will be a weapon that wipes out this cancer in our world."

He walked over to Doctor Kimiko and said something in Japanese. She shook her head quickly. The Oyabun walked back to me. "Continue assisting the doctor, and you will be rewarded for your cooperation. You are right about one thing. The magic in your blood and the genius of the doctor will win the day." He looked directly at Kimiko. "There is something poetic about the end of the Kyūketsuki being brought about by my own granddaughter."

# CHAPTER 18

"That could have gone better," the doctor announced, not looking at me as we walked out of the meeting. She was marching down the smooth cement floor of the parking garage, and I had to hurry to keep up.

"Yeah, we could be trying to save people instead of trying to wipe them out."

"People?" The doctor sighed. "You still don't understand." We walked down the long corridor, passing exotic black cars that belonged to the Yakuza. "Walt, you must stop thinking of these things as people. They lost their humanity long ago. They are predators."

I shot her a look, but she was ignoring me. "I've heard the same about the Yakuza." Was it me, or had the temperature in the parking garage dropped about twenty degrees? I looked at Harada, Ito, and Kimiko in turn. "But I never judged you. I gave you a chance. I have learned that the Yakuza are fierce, but so much more than that."

The doctor glared at me. "They're monsters, Walt."

"Who was it, Doctor? Who did they kill that brought you into this world?"

We got to the car, and Harada opened the door for us while Ito went to the driver's position. The doctor sat and looked out the window as I took my seat, and Harada closed our door. A moment later, the car started moving. She didn't look my way as she spoke. "My mother and father were taken from me when I was young. I will never forget that day. That was the day I dedicated my life to ending these parasites. My grandfather was behind me every step, and we both share this passion."

"I am sorry, Doctor Kimiko." I looked at her, hoping she'd look back. "If they could be cured, wouldn't you want that?"

She did turn my way, but there was steel in her eyes. "Finding a cure would be an incredible accomplishment, but the quality of your blood makes this impossible."

I sat back in my chair and looked out the window myself. "I don't believe that. I don't believe it's out of reach. I remember you saying that my blood has antigens that destroy the virus. That sounds like a giant step forward when it comes to finding a cure. More than anything, Doctor, I have absolute confidence in your ability. I know you can do this. If only you — "

"No," she interrupted. "We cannot separate the antigen from your t-cells. We know your DNA means the complete metabolic destruction of these creatures." She sat forward and wagged her head. "No, I will not alter our focus now. We have what we need, and when we can synthesize your DNA, we have the equipment needed to weaponize it. The days of the Kyūketsuki are numbered. Their extinction is assured."

"That is the will of the Yakuza, I understand. I can also understand wanting to eliminate the creatures that killed your parents. What I can't understand is why you cannot see that these vampires are so much more than just mindless monsters. They *remember*! They know who they are, and Kamenev told me that they have a complicated social hierarchy and network."

"Because you have spoken to that young female vampire in the fourth level, you think you know them? You do not, Walt."

This wasn't getting me anywhere. I decided to go in a different direction. "I know this is how the Yakuza takes care of enemies, but is the rest of the world on board with wiping them out? Isn't this genocide?"

The doctor gave me a small smile and went back to looking out the window. "It is not genocide any more than killing cockroaches in a kitchen. They are not a race or a people. They are an infection that seeks to spread and someday rule." She looked at me and tilted her head. "And yes, the rest of the world is behind our efforts. Anyone we've informed has approved."

"Really? I'm not sure that you are being completely forthcoming with all the information. I'm sure they know that I'm death on two legs for those who are infected, but I doubt they know my immune system kills the virus."

There was an awkward silence. She glared at me, and I wondered if she was ever going to speak. "What leads you to believe we have been withholding information?" she finally asked, tilting her head back to look down her nose at me.

I smirked at her. "Well, I'm starting to think that you haven't been completely honest with Kamenev."

Her eyes narrowed slightly at the mention of the Russian's name. "What makes you think that?"

"I think you know."

She never got a chance to answer. The car came to a quick stop, and we jerked forward. The doctor turned and barked something at the men in front. At a guess, it sounded like we were involved in some minor accident in the city.

"Walt! Move away from the windows and be still." the doctor said to me, pointing to the center of the limousine. "This could be an attack."

"Right," I answered.

She turned back to see what was happening up front. Perfect! I grabbed the handle of the door to my right and opened it. I was halfway out when I heard the doctor scream, "No!" as I bolted towards the front of the car.

Harada was opening his door, so I pushed it closed again as I passed his side. I saw an old lady thumping the front of the limousine with an umbrella. She was wearing a surgical mask and shrieking something at Ito as he got out of the driver's seat. He ran at me, and she jumped right in the way, still yelling.

I joined the sea of humanity crossing the street and stayed low. I was taller than most of the people around me, but I was pleased to see a lot of them also wearing blue suits. When we got to the end of the street, I ran about twenty feet and cut down an alley. I didn't look back as I ran with everything I had. My stupid dress shoes slapped the pavement, and all I heard was the sound of my own breathing, loud in my ears.

When I hit another main street, I took a hard right and ran for a few more minutes. I was done! I found a small newsstand to hide behind and catch my breath. I bent at the waist and put my hands on my knees, taking deep, ragged breaths. I straightened out when I could and looked both ways down the street. No sign of Harada, Ito, or the good doctor. *I was free.*

Standing on a street in Japan, I had no money, no contacts, and no idea where I was. Probably should have been more nervous, but I did have one thing going for me. I knew exactly where I had to go and what I had to do when I got there.

# CHAPTER 19

Tokyo was confusing. Everyone was going somewhere, and I stuck out like a sore thumb. I eventually found a couple of teenage girls who were more than happy to practice their English on me. There was a lot of giggling, but they did help me find what I needed. They showed me on their phone where I needed to go. It was quite a hike.

What bothered me most was not the walking but the fact that I didn't have much time. How long before Kimiko instructed Harada and Ito to let the Yakuza know I was on the run? What kind of time did I have before the Yakuza spread the word and I was caught?

Another thought made its way into my mind. What about the vampires? If they knew I was out in the open, exposed…best not think about that. Far better to get to my destination. Anything that happened after that didn't really matter. I was alone in every way that mattered, and that needed to change.

The signs were all in Japanese. I didn't know if I was looking at a store that sold phones or underwear. If I was right, I'd know my destination because there would be characters on the sign that would not be in Japanese. After about an hour and a half of walking, I saw a sign that had the flag I was looking for. The embassy. Bingo!

I walked in through the revolving doors and past a couple of armed guards who watched every step I took. Further into the building, I saw an older woman behind a huge desk. Her hair was drawn back in a dark bun, and she was all business as I walked up to her. "I am Suzana. May I help you?" she asked, with a voice that was lower than I expected. It was a relief to hear English again and know I would be understood.

"Yes, I have some information that I must give to the ambassador."

"Are you a citizen?" she asked, narrowing her eyes at me.

"No," I answered, looking at the floor.

"Perhaps you are in the wrong place." She wore a prim smile, probably happy to be sending me on my way.

"My name is Walt Baranov, and your ambassador will know who I am."

She shook her head. "I am sorry, you must make an appointment, or at the very least be a citizen to see the ambassador."

I held up my hands. "I understand, really. I don't have to see him, and you don't have to break a single rule. But I have information that is important. You have no idea!"

She didn't look convinced. "What are you asking?" she pressed with an eyebrow arched.

I saw a pad of paper and a pen beside it. I pointed to them and gave her my best smile. "A note. I can write a note. You can give this to the ambassador at his convenience, and he will be happy to get it."

Suzana studied me, considering my proposal. She finally shrugged and slid the pad and pen in front of me. "I will have to read your note to ensure it is... appropriate. You understand this, of course?"

I just nodded as I wrote. After putting my name on one side of the paper, I flipped it over and wrote nine words and who the message was for. I gave the note to Suzana and waited for her to read it.

She frowned and looked up at me. "Mister Baranov, this makes no sense, and I do not know the man who is to receive the note."

"That's okay!" I said quickly. "The ambassador will know exactly who that man is, and it's in code. It doesn't mean anything to you or anyone else reading it." I chuckled. "In fact, I'll bet that when you tell the ambassador who dropped it off, he'll be pretty interested in forwarding it to the right person. Can you do this for me?"

She nodded slowly. "Very well. This I can do."

"Thank you so much," I said and turned to leave.

"Wait! Mister Baranov, is there a number or address at which you can be reached?"

I put my hands in my pockets and looked at the floor. I looked up at her with a smile. "No, Suzana. I'm just waiting for the Yakuza to find me, and I have no idea where they're going to put me after I'm caught."

Her eyes widened at that. "Mister Baranov, are you in danger?"

"Oh, for sure," I said with a laugh and started heading for the door. I could hear her calling my name as I walked out. I was glad the guards didn't say anything as I left. They were still giving me the eye, but I didn't pose a threat to anyone. If Suzana wanted me stopped by force, she could have made that happen. That was a big decision to make, and she wasn't ready to make it. At least she was sharp enough to realize I meant every word I said, and that piece of paper was sure to get a reaction.

Back on the streets of Tokyo, I was at a loss. Relieved I hadn't been caught before I found the embassy, I didn't really care what happened next. I started walking back the way I came. There was no need to be inconspicuous or hide in any way. I felt many Japanese people walking by, giving me a glance but not staring right at me. Too polite for that.

I eventually got tired and wanted to sit down. I saw a dark alley with some wooden boxes piled a few feet in. Looked like a good place to rest, so I walked in and looked around. A few newspapers and a couple of squares of cardboard were on the ground, and it was dry. The noise of the street was barely audible in the little alley. It wasn't everyone's idea of comfort, but it looked pretty good to me.

I kicked a square of cardboard closer to the boxes and sat on it. I leaned against the wooden boxes, hugged myself, and closed my eyes. The hustle and bustle of the street sounded almost like waves. It was a white noise that helped me relax. I don't know if it was because of all the blood that was drawn or the excitement of the meeting, but I dozed off quickly.

There's no way for me to know how long I was out, but I woke to the feeling of a small impact on my shoe. I looked up to see Harada, Ito, and four other sour faces looking down at me. "You come now!" Harada barked as they grabbed me and hauled me to my feet.

"Nice to see you too, guys. Did you miss me?"

No response from the Yakuza heavies as they guided me to a van. The doors opened from within, and I was chucked in like a bag of laundry. There was no doctor to talk to and nothing to see after they put a bag on my head and handcuffed me. I had a pretty good idea of where they were taking me. Now, it was just a matter of waiting to see if I'd had any success at the embassy. "Get it done, Suzana," I said to myself.

# CHAPTER 20

Chained to a chair…again. This was becoming a habit. I think I liked the one in Kamenev's office better than the one in my old room back at Kimiko's facility. The Russian chair had a little more cushion and more angle in the backrest. Better view.

I'd been freaked out when I was sitting in that office, but at least I knew I hadn't done anything wrong. Oh sure, having Moscow cops find me with a dead girl who had melted was not a good thing. But I knew that I didn't do a damn thing wrong, and that had to come to light sooner or later.

This was different. I mean, I knew a lot more than the day things had first gone sideways, and I had done a lot since then. I was wondering how long it would take for that hornet's nest I kicked to come back at me. No way to know.

The door opened, and it was Kimiko. I couldn't see her, but I knew the sound of those heels. She came to stand in front of me, and the bag came off my head. She was wearing that white lab coat and an expression that could lower the temperature in hell. Yeah, she was pissed.

She crouched and looked me right in the eye. "Is this how you want it to be, Walt?" she whispered. "Manacled to a chair? Bled daily until we can make our own version of what you have? Your escape was a pointless waste of time and resources."

I gave her a smirk. "I'm fine with it, but we'd better figure out a bathroom schedule. It's not going to be me who's going to have to clean things up."

She straightened up and looked down her nose at me. "Maybe we don't clean it up at all. Have you considered that?"

I looked up and gave a small shrug. "Guess I'd better limit my eating and drinking. You might as well cancel dinner if that's the way it's going to be. If I die before you can make your own version of my blood, that's really going to make things difficult."

She tilted her head to one side. I swear she was considering giving me a slap. "As much as I would like to see Harada and Ito force-feed you, this would benefit nobody."

I laughed and looked away from her face. "Ah, well. Thanks for dropping by, Doctor. If you'll excuse me, I have a busy day of sitting ahead of me. I'd like to get back to it. Bye!"

I was sure I was getting a slap for that one, but

instead, she started undoing the chains and freeing me. "You have something else to do today, Walt. Sitting chained to a chair can continue another time."

"Ah, what's on my social itinerary today, Doctor? Another ride in the limousine? Board games with the Oyabun? Hot yoga?"

"Another teleconference has been requested."

I rubbed my wrists to ease the discomfort from the shackles. "You don't say? Any particular reason why?"

She glared at me. "I am told it is a routine conversation about our progress."

"Yeah, that's what I'd say, too." I laughed, rubbing my ankles when the shackles came off.

The doctor walked closer to me and folded her arms over her chest. "What do you mean by that? What do you believe is the purpose of this meeting?"

I sat back in my chair and grinned at her. "That's exactly what I would say if I was curious or had some suspicions about what you're doing here."

She lowered herself again to look into my eyes. I know it's stupid, but she was even more beautiful when she was mad. "What did you do, Walt?"

It was my turn to glare at her. "I did what needed to be done."

Harada walked in and said something in Japanese. The doctor nodded and walked to the television, grabbed the two lapel mics, and hooked us both up. The screen came alive, Harada walked out of the room, and we waited.

The screen flickered, and the two faces we'd come to expect split the screen, Agent Foster on the left and Ivan Kamenev on the right. Foster was frowning, while Kamenev looked…different. He was staring at us, and his eyes were red. *Tired!* That was it! He looked tired and a little stressed.

Foster spoke up first. "Greetings, Walt, Doctor. Thank you for this quick meeting. We're wondering about your progress. We're getting a lot of questions about this from other administrations and officials in our own country. Answers are what we need right now. What is your projected date of completion?"

The doctor nodded. "We are seven to ten days away from synthesizing Mister Baranov's DNA. Half as many days later, we should be able to have a number of delivery systems. The moment many of us have waited for is almost here."

"Good, that's good," Foster announced. "Are things well with you, Walt? How are you holding up?"

The doctor whirled to look at me, and her eyes were a little wide. I think she was holding her breath. "I'm doing great. Doctor Kimiko has been very kind, and she's even taken me on a quick tour of Tokyo. Amazing culture here. A great learning experience."

"Sightseeing? Is that wise, Doctor?" Kamenev asked.

She blinked at me a couple of times and recovered. "Yes, we felt it best for his mental health to show him some of the world he is saving. Motivation is important for his well-being."

"Agreed," Foster interjected.

"The risk," Kamenev said with a slight shake of his head. "We are hearing the vampires are afraid, and they know that they are in great danger. That fear will make them desperate. We must put caution above all. Walt must stay in your facility until the research is completed."

"I agree with you, Comrade," said the doctor, turning from the screen to me. She spoke again. "After which, we will hide him in another country until the conflict is resolved. When we can synthesize his DNA, we won't have need of him, but he will still be in danger. The vampires will not know our progress and seek to kill him."

Kamenev snorted a laugh. "That is no way to repay what Walt has done for us and the world. He is welcome to be my guest in Russia. He will be safe."

Foster raised a hand. "That's fine with us. Few have maintained secrecy better than our friend in Moscow. Are you up for that, Walt?"

I smiled at Kamenev. "As long as I get some more of Svetlana's tea, I'm in!"

The two men on the screen laughed. The doctor held up a hand to speak. "If that is satisfactory, I would like to close this meeting and resume my duties."

Kamenev held up a hand of his own. "There is another matter I must address before we adjourn."

"Very well," Foster conceded. "What's on your mind, Comrade Kamenev?"

The Russian held up a piece of paper. "This note was delivered to the Russian Embassy in Tokyo. I need some further explanation."

My heart sang. If Kamenev is holding up the note...*he came to Japan to get it.* Things were looking good. Really good!

The doctor froze. "I know nothing of this note."

"You would not," Kamenev explained. "Mister Baranov was the one to write and deliver this message." He unfolded the paper and looked at it. He shook his head and looked right at me. "Walt, how could you possibly have this information? How can you know this?"

I could feel all their eyes on me. "There's only one way I could know what is on that paper. I think you know that, Mister Kamenev."

The man from Moscow nodded and wore a tight-lipped smile. "If Agent Foster has no objection, I would like a private conversation with Walt. Would that be acceptable, Doctor Kimiko?"

She shot me a look of death over her shoulder and smiled sweetly at the screen. "I have no objection."

Foster just shrugged. "Fine with me."

"Very good," Kamenev replied. "Until we talk again, friends."

"Signing off," Foster declared, and his side of the screen went blank.

"I will excuse myself as well," the doctor said, looking at Kamenev and then me. She turned, and her heels tapped on the tiles as she left the room.

The Russian's face took up the entire screen. He looked down at the note and then up at me. "Please explain, Walt. How can this be?"

I held up both my hands. "It IS true, Mister Kamenev. You don't think it was a lucky guess that you had a family dog, and her name was Boris...*do you*?"

# CHAPTER 21

He narrowed his eyes at me. "This is something you heard from Elena before she attacked, yes?"

I wracked my brain, but I just couldn't think of a way to break it to the old guy gently. "No, Irina told me."

I heard him suck in a breath through his teeth. "You have seen her?"

"Yeah, I can see her whenever I want. She's one of the test subjects imprisoned in the fourth sublevel of this nuthouse."

His eyes bulged. "*Vot eto pizdets!*" I didn't know a lot of Russian, but I recognized that little bit of profanity. I didn't really blame him.

"Oh yes, there are vampires from all over the world in the basement of this facility. I'm sorry to tell you that Irina is one of them."

The man gritted his teeth and shook his head. I couldn't imagine what must have been going through his mind. "This changes nothing. It may be Irina, but she is a vampire now. She is lost to us."

"That's just it, Mister Kamenev. I think she is very much in there. I think the vampires of the world are victims of their condition. The people who work here are not focused on learning about them. They only see them half-starved in a cell. When they need to feed, they aren't thinking straight. After that thirst is solved, they can talk. They can reason."

Kamenev was silent as he mulled it over. "What are you asking me, Walt?"

I looked at the ground and shook my head. "I want to keep talking to Irina, find out how much she can remember. I'm asking you to put some pressure on this facility to find a cure. Find a way to destroy the virus, not wipe out everyone that has it. I mean, at least explore the possibility."

The man nodded slowly. "I see. Anything else?"

"Well, it would be nice if they stopped chaining me to this chair."

Kamenev scowled. "I think it's time I visited this 'facility' just to see how things work."

This was too much to hope for. "You think... you think the Yakuza would permit that?"

The Russian laughed. "Oh, Walt. I never know what you will say next. The Yakuza must be treated with respect, and they are indeed a threat. However, when I want to visit a facility that Russia has helped to bankroll, I will not be denied. They know I will arrive in a car or in a tank."

***

I walked out of the room to see the doctor, flanked by Harada and Ito. "You visited the Russian Embassy?" the doctor asked, staring at me.

"Wasn't easy, but yeah, I found it."

"What did Kamenev want?"

"Well, let's see. He wanted to know how I knew the name of the family dog. He wasn't too happy to hear that I was a prisoner, but I think what really pissed him off was finding out his daughter is being held on the fourth sublevel."

The three of them looked like they'd been struck by lightning. "His daughter?"

I smiled. "Yes, cell number twenty. The girl. She looked familiar, as I accidentally killed her mother. You really didn't know?"

The doctor shook her head, speechless.

"Oh, well, I don't think he liked that. Anyway, he says he's coming here to look around."

Kimiko's eyes widened. "He is coming to Japan?"

"No, he's already in Japan. He's probably calling your Oyabun right now. Said he'd arrive in a car...or a tank."

Harada and Ito looked at each other quickly while the doctor put her hands on her hips. "Where do you think you're going?"

"I'm hungry. Going to get another one of those

steaks." I looked at Harada. "I'll find you when I'm finished eating. I'd like to spend some more time with Irina." I turned and walked away, leaving the three of them to panic in silence.

# CHAPTER 22

I was almost done with my steak, and I didn't mind sitting alone one bit. I wasn't good company, and I didn't see the facility around me the same way anymore. Same with the people who worked here. The busy cafeteria had people sitting in groups, and I was the only one eating alone. I could still feel them staring at me and talking in hushed tones. I didn't know if I was the subject of their conversations, and I didn't care.

I was having a big slug of water and thinking about going back for some dessert when she sat down at my table. "Oh, hello, Doctor Kimiko. You hungry too?"

She took off her glasses and set them on the table. She looked me in the eyes, and I thought I'd melt. "I've come to talk to you, Walt." I noticed she was talking softly, and her tone was different, kinder.

"Don't you want to chain me to a chair first?"

The lovely doctor let out a sigh and nodded.

"I deserve that. We...we overreacted to your escape in Tokyo. We could not believe the answer that we found with your discovery. The fear of losing that opportunity caused us to take steps that we should not have taken." She reached out and took my hand. "I'm sorry, Walt. Please forgive us."

I put down my fork and sighed, too. "Okay, Doctor. Okay. But please, no more chains and handcuffs. Alright?"

She nodded and smiled. "Some men in Tokyo pay large sums of money to be handcuffed by a woman."

I couldn't help snorting out a laugh. "Oh my God! Was that a joke, Doctor?"

She laughed, too. "Am I so cold and without emotion?"

"Most of the time," I said with a shrug. "It's cool. That's your job."

She let go of my hand and tapped the table with a finger. "That is not the only thing I need to discuss. I've come to put your mind at ease."

"About what?"

She put on her glasses, sat back in her chair, and tented her fingers on the table. "Why a cure for this virus is impossible, and weaponizing your DNA is our only option."

I sat back, too. "Okay, help me understand."

"You are not wrong about your blood containing antigens that attack the virus."

"See, that's what I mean," I said with a frown. "I thought when someone beats a virus, their body creates antibodies that can defeat it. Right?"

She pointed a finger at me and returned it to her arm. "You're right. Normally, that would give us a huge opportunity to create more antibodies, and a cure would indeed be found."

"You said, 'normally,' so what's the issue?"

She placed her hands on the table and looked at me. "See, your t-cells, the things that create these antibodies, also have your DNA written on them. Do you remember me telling you what your DNA does to that of the infected?"

I nodded. "Yeah, my DNA pulls the altered DNA apart, right?"

"Yes!" she almost cheered. "If we were to inject your antibodies into a vampire, the virus would indeed be destroyed."

I closed my eyes and let out a groan. "As well as every single cell in their body. They'd melt into a puddle of goo."

Her face tilted to one side, and she gave me a sad smile. "So you see, my hands are tied. There is no viable way to create a cure at this point. There remains one solution to this problem."

"Okay, Doctor. I see where I'm wrong. Are you ready to find out the truth about the people who have been infected? Are you ready to open your mind and see what I have seen?"

Her hand came to her chin, and she rubbed it as she considered my offer. "Okay, Walt. I must say you have piqued my interest."

I looked at my old watch. "It's almost feeding time. Come down with me and don't let her see you're there. Just listen to us talk. See if you don't come away with a new point of view."

"Very well, Walt. I will come and listen one day." She got up from the table. "Please excuse me. We are expecting the arrival of Mister Kamenev any minute, and I should be there to greet him."

I got up, too. "Do you mind if I come? I'd like to see that guy again. I really owe him."

"If you are finished eating, you are welcome to accompany me."

I got up, joined her, and we walked out of the large cafeteria. As much as I was looking forward to seeing my Russian friend, I worried about how this could affect him. I know how it affected me.

# CHAPTER 23

It was something to see, let me tell you, watching Kamenev stroll into the facility with six of the biggest men in suits. They would make a Russian bear tremble! Some had a couple of neck tattoos that made them look even more sinister. It looked like the edge of a Russian star was poking out from their collars.

The Oyabun of the Yakuza was surrounded by smaller men in suits, but there were more of them. Henchmen, foot soldiers, to be sure. Harada and Ito were there as well. The boss wore his usual elegant white suit.

As scary as these two groups were, they came together, and there was nothing but respect demonstrated by both of the big men. Kamenev bowed first and deep, and the Oyabun returned it smartly. Then they came and shook hands like old friends. Afterward, they acknowledged the Doctor and then me.

I saw something in Kamenev's eyes. The man was worried and stressed, and I had to feel sorry for him. Imagine losing a daughter only to find out she was a test subject in a facility that studies vampires. I regretted telling him, but there was no other way to get any weight to my cause.

The doctor led us into a boardroom, and everyone sat down. The heavies all waited outside. I wondered what they did while the big bosses talked. Glare at each other? Flex their muscles? Tell jokes? No idea.

My immediate concern was the meeting. Kamenev was the first to speak. "Young Walt has communicated to me that he believes a cure for this virus is attainable. Up until now, we have only considered his discovery to be a means to destroy our enemies. Killing such vermin would give me great pleasure, but to cure these people, to give them back their lives, would that not be a greater accomplishment?"

The Oyabun looked at Kimiko, his face made of stone. The doctor nodded and answered the Russian. "As I have recently explained to Walt, there is no cure in sight. While Walt's blood and immune system does indeed produce antigens that destroy the virus, it is his DNA that makes a cure impossible."

Kamenev glanced at me and then back to the doctor. "Please, go on."

She smiled and looked back at me as she spoke. "Walt's DNA reacts violently with the DNA that has been rewritten by the virus. Remember, when a person is bitten by someone who has been infected, the virus starts its work. It begins altering the DNA, the very building blocks of the person, immediately. It adds some things and removes others. After twelve hours of infection, the patient loses the ability to produce their own blood cells to sustain them. They acquire acute senses and changes in their anatomy, and they barely age. They become predators who only care about self-preservation."

The Russian tented his fingers on the table. "And killing the virus will not undo these major changes to the person infected, am I right?"

"That's not the issue," the doctor said with a shake of her head. "Their DNA would react, implode really before the antigens had a chance to do their job. Walt's antigens carry his DNA signature, and for reasons that we don't really understand, they will cause a metabolic meltdown in whomever receives this 'cure.' I am sorry, Comrade Kamenev. You have come a long way for nothing."

"Not for nothing, it would seem." Kamenev looked at me and then back at the doctor. "I have a chance to see my daughter one last time. You cannot put a price on such a thing." He leaned forward and glared at the woman across from him. "I must ask… *did you know?*"

Doctor Kimiko swallowed and looked at the table. "I swear, I did not know that subject number twenty is your daughter."

I held up a hand quickly. This was getting ugly. "Mister Kamenev, I believe her on this. I really do. It was just a weird coincidence that I could figure it out. Dumb luck, really."

"Explain," the Oyabun said quietly.

"Ah, well...this weird thing in my blood was discovered when I was bitten in Russia. The woman who bit me just happened to be Mister Kamenev's wife." The Oyabun and Doctor Kimiko's eyebrows shot up, and they looked at each other. "I will regret forever that I was responsible for her death," I said, looking at the Russian.

Kamenev nodded his understanding at me. "My daughter was the image of her mother. I am not surprised you were able to detect the resemblance."

"That was the only way," I agreed. "If I had not...uh...if I hadn't seen Elena, there's no way I would have put it together. There is no way our friends in Japan could have known. Irina isn't exactly talkative in her present state."

"And that brings us to the final part of this meeting," Kamenev said. "Walt, if it's not too much trouble, could you please take me to my daughter?"

# CHAPTER 24

We walked out of the boardroom, Kamenev first, me following, and then the doctor and Oyabun. As soon as we got near the bodyguards, Oyabun said something quickly to Harada. "Hai!" he agreed quickly and fell in step behind me and the guest from Russia.

We walked by the many different employees in this facility, and they averted their eyes and scuttled past. Not like before, where they would inspect me and discuss my presence when they felt I was out of earshot. Oh no! They were terrified of Kamenev, and it was weird that I wasn't. I knew he was tough, but he'd never been anything but kind to me. I mean, I accidentally killed the guy's wife. In a weird way, that gave us a deeply personal connection. Perhaps we understood each other's pain.

The escalators took us down to the dreaded fourth sublevel. I saw one of the workers, a small Japanese man wearing his hair in a ponytail. He bowed at us and ran away. Kamenev ignored his greeting, but I gave a small wave of acknowledgement. "Mister Kamenev, I've got to warn you, she's not at her best right now. You're not interested in waiting until after she's fed?"

The Russian's jaw set, but his eyes were kind as he looked at me. "This is a chance for me to see her one last time. I am under no illusions, Walt. I know what this damned virus does to people."

I knew he meant every word, but to see your daughter infected, filthy, and crazy…that was going to be hard. I suddenly wished I was anywhere else. "Do you want me to wait here, Mister Kamenev?"

He shook his head. "No. Bring me to her, Walt. One last chance to see my beautiful girl."

"Here," I said, pointing. "Cell number twenty." I walked to the intercom button and pressed it. "Irina, it's me, Walt. There…there is someone here to see you."

Kamenev came up beside me and peered into the cell, searching. "It is empty?"

"Wait," I cautioned him as I pressed the button again. "Irina, please come out from under the bed."

A hiss came from the speaker above us, and there was some movement under the bunk. One delicate and dirty hand reached out and placed a palm on the tiled floor. I pointed to the button. "Talk to her, Mister Kamenev. She will be herself for only a few seconds."

He took a breath and let it out slowly. His big hand moved forward, and he jammed a thumb into the button to communicate. "Irina, moya doch."

She emerged from under the bunk, those dark eyes wide. There was dried blood on her chin, and her filthy hair stuck to her head, some falling in front of her face. She stood up and looked right at the Russian. "*Papa, eto ty?*" she hissed.

The big man put a hand up and leaned his forehead against the glass. "Eto ya, eto ya!" he whispered as tears welled up in his eyes.

She took a couple of halting steps forward, one hand reaching out. A small rivulet from a tear of blood made its way down one cheek. She remembered!

The change happened fast. Her brows drew down, and she opened her mouth to expose a black tongue and sharp teeth. "*Idi syuda!*" she hissed and jumped at the glass. "*IDI SYUDA!*"

To his credit, Kamenev didn't budge. He closed his eyes and listened to the monster in the cell that only a moment ago had looked at him with recognition. That one look was everything, and it was gone. She was gone.

He sank to his knees, turning his back to the cell, and sat on the floor. His hands covered his face, and I could tell by the way he was breathing that he was weeping. He was quiet in his grief, but I couldn't stand to see the proud man so broken.

I sat down beside him on the floor and just stared at the ground. "Mister Kamenev, I am so sorry. Was I wrong to tell you about her?"

He put a hand on my knee and wiped his eyes with the other. We could still hear Irina raving behind the glass, but it was quieter now the intercom was off. "No, Walt. Just to see her, to remember my little dove. It is a gift. I thank you for that."

"If you could just wait until she's fed. There is much more clarity in her thoughts. She remembers who she is and the life she had."

"It is a life that is gone now, Walt." He shook his head slowly. "I must go. Irina must let go. These are her last days. Her nightmare is coming to an end."

We sat there for a while. Neither of us said anything. We didn't need to. When the big Russian had composed himself, he stood up and offered me a hand. I got to my feet, and we started walking out of the fourth level. "What will you do now?" I asked the man.

He shrugged. "I will inform my superiors that a cure is not possible and concentrate on preparing for our final offensive to remove this sickness from the world."

The two of us went up the escalator and found the Oyabun, his security, and Kamenev's team of no-necks waiting for us. The Russian turned to me, shook my hand, and turned his attention to the Oyabun. They started walking and talking with the two teams of security following them.

I watched them go and turned to walk back to my room. None of the employees even looked my way as I walked. I was old news, I guessed. I pushed open the door to my room, and it looked different.

There was a small bookshelf jammed full of reading material right beside my bed. Under the large television was a new DVD player and a stack of films arranged just under the screen. All the latest releases.

Just inside the door was a small table with a coffeemaker and a tin of cookies. But the most pleasant surprise was Doctor Kimiko, sitting on my bed with a small smile on her face. I raised an eyebrow, and she stood up. "That was a good thing you did, Walt."

"What? Telling Kamenev his daughter was here?"

She shook her head. "That was...necessary. I understand that." She walked very close to me, still wearing the smile. "No, telling our Russian ally that we could not possibly have known that subject twenty was his daughter. That was brilliant."

I frowned at the elegant woman, even as I was intoxicated by her delicate scent. "That has the virtue of being the truth. I don't believe you had a clue who she was in her past life."

"We did not. You defended the actions of this facility and the Oyabun. You saved him a tremendous amount of face. He is in your debt and has insisted you get anything you desire for the short amount of time you will be staying here." Her smile grew wider. "Anything you want, Walt."

I sat there blinking. I'd just watched a grown

man cry for the daughter he would never see again. I wasn't in the mood for anything but a quiet moment to get over that heartbreaking scene.

Her eyes grew wide as I walked around her and started making myself a drink with the newly arrived coffeemaker. "There are only a few things I'd like, Doctor." I turned and looked at her as the machine hissed and bubbled. "I'd like you to consider looking for a cure."

She sighed and looked down. "I have already explained why it cannot be done."

"No, you've explained why you *think* it can't be done. Just be open to another answer if it presents itself, okay? Is that too much to ask?"

Kimiko shook her head quickly. "No, it is not. What else can we do for you?"

I leaned against the table and crossed my arms. "I'd like to continue spending more time with Irina, and I want her to get three bags at feeding time. Can you do that?"

The doctor walked to me again. "This, I do not understand." She put a hand on my arm. "Walt, her days are numbered. There is nothing we can do for her. Do you understand this?"

I nodded. "Yes, but can you do it? Three bags at feeding time, and let me talk to her. Okay?"

She looked at me for a long time. I was about to ask again when she shrugged and spoke. "Very well, Walt. The Oyabun was very specific in his instruction.

You are to get what you want, and what you ask is not beyond our power."

"Good. Thanks, Doctor."

It was a bit awkward as neither of us said anything. There was nothing to say. She turned toward the door and paused halfway through the threshold. "Walt, why do you want to spend this time with her?"

I took a sip of my coffee and looked at my shoes. "Because she doesn't have anyone else."

The doctor didn't look like she was any closer to understanding, but she didn't press me for an explanation. She left and closed the door behind her.

"I don't have anyone, either," I whispered to the empty room.

# CHAPTER 25

We had a routine by now, and everyone was sticking to it. It was always the same. A gentle alarm would wake me in the morning. I'd use the bathroom, walk down to the serving area in my robe, and get my breakfast. I didn't care that nobody else was wearing a robe and pajamas. It wasn't long until nobody else cared either. I was pretty sure that everyone knew who I was and why I was there by now. The novelty was over.

I'd read or watch a movie, get dressed, and head down for lunch just after noon. As soon as I got back to my room, the doctor would be there with a nurse, and they'd harvest blood. They would take a lot of it.

The fatigue would hit, and then I'd nap until dinner. Again, the alarm would ring, I'd walk to the serving area, and a steak would be waiting for me. I'd add some vegetables and pick up a fruit drink to wash it all down. I'd eat alone. Always alone.

When the steak was finished and nothing was

on my plate, I'd head to the fourth floor, where Harada was waiting. I was really starting to like the guy. He would always greet me and stay out of the way while I interacted with Irina.

That was the highlight of my day. Wasn't easy watching her polish off three big bags of blood, but as soon as she did, what a difference! She'd look you in the eyes and listen. Her skin was nowhere near as pale.

We'd made a game of our communication. I borrowed an English/Russian dictionary and asked my questions in Russian. Irina would do her best to answer in my language. It wasn't easy, and it took a long time, but we had plenty of time and nothing else to do.

I found out she remembered her father, her mother, and even her grandfather. The sweetest thing was when she fumbled to explain their favorite activity. "*Dedushka, Grandfather would take me vishling,*" she said with a smile. Her voice still had a hollow tone.

"Vishling?" I asked.

She made a motion with her hand, a swimming motion as if through water. I grabbed my dictionary. "Oh!" I said, "Do you mean...uh...na rybalke? Fishing?"

Her head went back as she laughed, and she brought a hand to her mouth. "*Da! Fishing!*"

I laughed, too. "That's nice...uh...eto milo."

"*Da,*" she agreed. "*Ochen khorosho.*"

I felt Harada's hand on my arm. I looked at

him, and he was politely pointing at his watch. He was right, and I wish he wasn't. Time was up. The day they learned how to synthesize my blood, it was over for both of us. They'd use it on Irina, and I'd be sent home, wherever that was now.

"Proshchay, Irina," I said softly, putting a hand on the glass.

"*Goodbye, Walt,*" she answered. Her hand went up to mine. We'd look into each other's eyes, and I had a hard time turning from her. There was so much more I wanted to know, wanted to say. I heard Harada clear his throat politely. I got the message and turned away.

Probably the worst part of visiting Irina was saying goodbye and the long walk back to my room. Didn't matter how many people would walk by, I always felt completely isolated. I was surrounded by people and never more alone.

Harada would bid me goodnight, I'd do the same, and I'd be in my room. I read until I couldn't keep my eyes open and fell asleep. The alarm would wake me, and it would start all over again.

One morning, I was yawning on my way to breakfast when Doctor Kimiko fell in step with me. She was wearing a black skirt, matching shirt, and the usual white lab coat. Did she ever sleep?

"Good morning, Walt."

"Good morning, Doctor."

She looked me up and down and wore a smirk. "I see you are dressing for comfort rather than style."

I shrugged without looking at her. "I guess I value my comfort more than the opinion of the people who work here." I looked down at my bathrobe and gave her a small smile. "I like this robe, and the slippers aren't too bad. Maybe I can keep them when this is all over."

"That may be sooner than anticipated."

I stopped dead and looked at her. "Pardon?"

She clasped her hands behind her back and looked at me. She said the words I'd once wanted to hear but now dreaded. "We have had a successful trial synthesizing your blood. Your time here is almost done."

# CHAPTER 26

I stared at the oatmeal as I stirred it with my spoon. I didn't look at the doctor sitting across from me in the vast cafeteria. "How long?" I mumbled.

"Two to three days at the most," she answered and took a sip of her tea.

My spoon dug into the oatmeal, and I pulled it out. I blew on the steaming portion awaiting my mouth. "So what does that mean?"

"For you or for the test subjects?"

"Both."

The doctor moved her glasses slightly higher up her nose and looked at her tea as intently as I watched my oatmeal. "You will be kept as a safeguard until the tests are completed. We have every reason to believe that we have been successful in replicating the qualities of your blood. You must remain in the facility until we are certain that what we have produced can be weaponized. When that has been proven, you will be released into the country of your choosing to live in anonymity."

I shoveled the spoon of oatmeal into my mouth and chewed on her answer as I ate. "Okay, that's how my story ends. How will you be certain you've succeeded? What happens to the test subjects?"

"Ah," the doctor said, and turned the delicate cup around on the table with both hands. "We will test what we have created on the test subjects on level four. There are a number of ways we can weaponize your DNA and the antigens in your system. When we know what works, there will be a push to hunt down and eliminate these creatures."

I pushed the bowl away. I wasn't hungry. Not anymore. "How...how can you turn my DNA into a weapon? I mean, how is this done?"

She shrugged. "There are a few ways. For example, we have been experimenting with a type of bullet that is hollow. Your DNA is inserted into the center of this bullet."

"Like a jelly donut?" I offered.

"A what?"

"A donut. A pastry with jelly injected into it. You don't have them here?"

"I understand." The doctor nodded her head. "A dessert with a center that has been added." She stared at me. "You are an odd young man, Walt."

"That's true," I agreed. "How does the bullet work?"

"When it hits any living thing it will do damage. When it hits a vampire, it starts a catastrophic meltdown that results in certain death."

I frowned at her. "Well, that sounds horrible. How else are you weaponizing what you've taken out of me?"

Kimiko tapped one of her manicured nails on the table. "The one that shows the most promise is an airborne application. An aerosol."

I folded my arms on my chest and leaned back in my chair. "Like, a gas? You're joking."

"I am not. It has a wide dispersal, and we just need to understand how the concentration works."

"How do you send out a gas?"

She shook her head. "That's beyond my expertise. From what I understand, they plan on using drones of some kind. They will release the gas that contains your DNA, and once it comes in contact with any vampires—"

"Yeah, I get the idea," I interrupted. "And you mean to use these on the people on the fourth floor?"

She looked me in the eyes. "I must."

I looked down at the table and let out a sigh. I got it. Had to test it on the guinea pigs, and when they died horribly, that was all the evidence needed. Weapons that would destroy vampires on a massive scale would be used, and it would be over.

Two to three days. That was how long Irina had to live. That was how long I had to say goodbye. It wasn't enough, but there was nothing to be done. Fate had only given Irina and me one sweet, brief moment. That was all.

It was like the doctor read my mind. She reached out and took my hand. "Walt, I can ensure that subject twenty is the last to participate. I can do that much, but nothing more."

My sight grew blurry, and the hand that was free wiped my eyes. I nodded my thanks, and the doctor patted my hand and stood up. "I wish there was more I could do for you and for her. I am not as cold-blooded as you believe, Walt."

I looked up at the doctor and smiled at her. "I never thought you were cold, Doc. I think you're brilliant. I know you're passionate about solving this. We just have different ideas about how to do it."

She gave me a smile. A real smile. "I'm not drawing blood anymore. I don't need to do that at this stage of research. Spend what time you have left with the young woman, Walt." Without another word, she turned and walked away.

"That is a hell of a good idea, Kimiko," I said to myself.

# CHAPTER 27

Harada and I went down the escalator to the fourth floor. My impassive escort was silent and polite, like usual. It got to the point where I would forget he was there when I visited Irina. I'd find him, he'd follow me, and then he stayed inconspicuous. I appreciated that.

We went by that same worker with the ponytail as we walked the hall on the sublevel. He didn't greet me in any way, and I got the impression that Harada didn't like that. My usually silent partner grunted something at him in Japanese. Didn't sound complimentary, but it was none of my business.

The other cells were quiet. I didn't see any of the test subjects moving. Seemed odd that they were all resting. Pablo was usually glowering at whoever came down to that floor, but I didn't see him at all. I got to cell twenty and looked in the glass. I couldn't see Irina, but that was expected. I looked at my watch and knew things were about to change.

Sure enough, a bell sounded, and the three bags of blood fell from the hatch in the ceiling. I looked at the bunk and saw Irina crawl out. She pounced on the bags and fed. It was hard to watch, not because she was wolfing down blood, but because she needed it so badly. I knew her own body couldn't make the blood cells she needed. Not anymore.

I put my hand on the glass and gave a light tap. "Irina!" I called, not even using the intercom. She was hissing as she turned to face me, and then her face transformed. She blinked a couple of times, and she smiled. It was amazing to watch her skin go from pale to pink. No less amazing to watch her mind return and recognize me. "*Walt!*" her hollow, haunting voice called out. "*You are early, nyet?*"

Her English was improving a lot faster than my Russian. Was that also a symptom of the virus? If every other sense became more acute, could her ability to learn also improve? I pressed the button to be heard a little better and looked at some papers I'd put in the dictionary I had brought. "Hey, Irina. Priyezzhayut syuda chasto?"

She laughed, the oddest sound. It was high-pitched, but it sounded like it was coming from a tin can. Probably because of the intercom. "*Yes, Walt. I do come here often.*"

We both laughed. She put her hand up against the glass, mirroring mine. I guess it was her version of holding hands. It made me smile, and it broke my heart. I looked at the bags on the floor. "Feel better after feeding?"

She shook her head, shrugged, and frowned.

"Oh!" I flipped a few more pages and found what I was looking for. "Ty chuvstvuyesh' sebya luchshe posle yedy?" My pronunciation was brutal, but she seemed to understand.

"*Da, better. No angry.*"

"Your voice sounds stronger, too." I looked at the book again. Seemed like forever before I found my next words. "Tvoy golos khoroshiy."

Irina gave me a sly look. "*You like voice? Come inside and hear.*"

"Nyet! Uh…nyet! Bad idea! You don't want me anywhere near you, Irina. Dover'tes' mne!"

She put her other hand on the glass. "*Trust? I trust Walt. Yedinstvennyy!*"

Our conversation was interrupted by gunfire that made us both jump. Harada had his automatic pistol out and was firing shot after shot. I saw a shadow jump out of the darkness and take the Japanese guard to the ground.

I recognized the assailant as Pablo, the old Spaniard from the first cell. He was out, and he wasn't alone. Three other forms came running around the corner, screaming and hissing. One looked ancient and was bald, his teeth exposed and saliva dripping down his chin. The other two were younger and smaller. They had long, dark hair, and they all wore hospital gowns.

The first got to me and grabbed my throat with one hand. Big mistake! He came away with a bubbling stump. The other two stopped screaming and watched the vampire who touched me start to dissolve. They looked back at me, but it was too late.

I threw a punch at the closest creature and felt my knuckles smack into its eye. Both of its hands clapped on its face as it fell away from me and began to come apart. The last vampire roared at me. I roared back and clapped a hand on its forehead. The skull sank in right away, and there was a thud as its body hit the floor.

I ran to where I saw Harada go down. Pablo was on top of him, feeding. "NO!" I screamed, smacked my hands on either side of his head, and squeezed. I felt the skin start to bubble, and the skull gave way as the old faker screamed his last. I used my grip on what was left of his head to throw him to the side and looked down at the man who had been my escort since I arrived.

Harada looked bad. He was pale and bleeding from the throat where Pablo had bitten him. I couldn't understand a word he was saying. I put pressure on the wound with my hands. He was reaching for his gun. I looked around and didn't see any other creatures out. Why did he need the gun?

Then it hit me. It was to use it on himself! I kicked it away and called for help. I heard Irina screaming, too. "*Syn meduzy!*" she called. "*Walt, ty syn meduzy!*"

Harada was bitten and wanted to die, and Irina was going crazy. I didn't know what to do, so I just kept calling. I looked back at Irina. She was crying blood and pointing at me. Again, she called, "*Syn meduzy!*"

Now she knew. I was the story that the vampires would tell to frighten each other. I was the one they feared and dreaded. Medusa's son.

# CHAPTER 28

People were everywhere. The fourth level, usually deserted, was jammed with workers from the facility. Some were wearing suits, probably Yakuza soldiers. Others were dressed like medical personnel and wore masks. I kneeled on the floor over Harada, and I was found by a frantic Doctor Kimiko.

She started talking in Japanese to me and quickly switched to English. "Walt! Are you harmed?"

"No, but Harada was bitten!" I gestured with my head to show her who I was helping. He was still lying down, and I was still putting pressure on the wound. He said something in Japanese to the doctor, and she replied. Harada repeated himself, and she shook her head. Harada was asking for something, and she wasn't having it.

"What does he want? Is he thirsty or something?"

"He wants to die," she explained.

I turned and looked at him and then at the

doctor. "He's wounded, but if he gets some blood put back and some stitches…"

"You misunderstand." The doctor clasped her hands in front of her. "Walt, he prefers death to what comes next."

"Is he going to…" I let it hang in the air. I didn't want to say it out loud in front of Harada.

"The virus will either kill him or turn him at this point. There is nothing to be done about that," the doctor explained.

A gurney arrived, and two small men in white uniforms lifted the moaning Harada onto the apparatus and rolled him away. Ito approached us and looked around at the carnage. He went to one knee and inspected the puddles of gore that used to be Pablo and the other three vampires. Ito said something to Kimiko, and she nodded. He looked at me and gave me a tight-lipped smile of approval.

The doctor touched my arm. "Please excuse me. I must attend to Harada. I must do what I can for him."

Ito and I watched her go. I walked over to cell twenty and looked for Irina. She was under the bunk, and she had left her blanket in the middle of the cell. She'd seen everything, and I wondered if she would ever leave her hiding place again.

A couple of Yakuza in dark suits had the small Asian man with the ponytail in their grasp. He looked at me as they carried him past. "Gaijin inu ga shinu!" he growled at me. Ito slapped him hard the moment the words came out of his mouth. That shut him up.

Ito looked at me. "He let Kyūketsuki out of cage to kill you."

I watched as they threw him into Pablo's old cell. "What will happen to him?" I asked. The Yakuza foot soldier spat on the ground. "He has chosen the Kyūketsuki. He will become one of them and die." He walked past me and left me alone on the fourth floor.

I looked at the little worker in his cell. I walked up to him, and he started swearing at me in Japanese. I shook my head and pressed the intercom button to speak. "You don't betray the Yakuza, dumbass!" I turned my back on him and walked away. I needed a drink.

***

I asked for a rum and coke, but I didn't think I'd actually get one. This place was full of surprises. I took a big pull and stared straight ahead. Somewhere, Harada was suffering. He was begging for death rather than facing the dishonor of turning into a vampire. Did it hurt? The change from an ordinary person into one of those things...was it painful?

I made a mental note to ask the doctor what the transformation was like for anyone infected. The virus would be rewriting his DNA, and I had no idea how much pain was involved in that process. Harada would just have to deal with it until the twelve hours expired. After that, he would die like all the others when my DNA was released into the world. I stood up fast, and my glass skipped across the table and smashed on the floor, sending a puddle of rum and coke oozing in its wake. *Twelve hours!*

People stared as I ran out of the massive cafeteria. If they'd known what I was about to do, they would have followed me.

# CHAPTER 29

I ran down the halls, only stopping people to ask where I could find Doctor Kimiko. If they didn't have an answer, I just kept running. I didn't care who I was scaring, and I didn't care if they thought I was nuts. Time was the only thing that mattered now, and it mattered to everyone in this crazy mess.

Finally, a couple of orderlies offered to show me. They started walking, and I grabbed one by the arm. "We've got to hurry! It's important!"

They started hustling. This was a good break, and I hoped I could get a few more. I needed some luck, for me, for everyone.

Eventually, they brought me to a hospital wing, and I saw the doctor walking with a surgical mask behind a large glass window. She was wearing her lab coat and writing on her clipboard, Harada in front of her. His skin was grey and had a sheen of perspiration. There were dark circles around his sunken eyes. He looked like crap.

I banged on the glass to get her attention. She wheeled on one heel and stared at me. I couldn't see her mouth, but her eyes said it all. Kimiko was frowning at me like I was interrupting.

"I need to talk to you!" I shouted at the glass. She motioned for me to walk further down the hall. I did as she instructed and found a door.

Kimiko was waiting with a surgical mask. She opened the door and handed me the mask. "Don't say a word until this is on," she ordered.

I tied the damn thing on and started. "Doctor! I have an idea! I think we can save Harada!"

She folded her arms on her chest and stuck out one hip. "Harada is beyond help. I am merely trying to make him comfortable as he transitions. It is a unique opportunity to study the virus as it progresses."

"He doesn't have to die! He doesn't have to change!" I explained.

"What are you talking about, Walt?"

I took a deep breath and let it out to settle myself. "I want to show you something. If I'm right, you'll see things my way."

The doctor slowly nodded her agreement. I walked over to Harada and reached out a hand.

"Walt! You must not!"

I looked at her and held up a hand. "I know what I'm doing. Well...I'm pretty sure I'm right." I turned back to the unconscious Harada. "One way to find out."

I placed my hand gently on the man's forehead. His skin felt hot and clammy. Nothing happened at first, but then Harada gasped and opened his eyes. He said something weakly in Japanese and was breathing hard.

The doctor grabbed my arm and removed it from the patient's head. Neither of us expected what we saw. There, on Harada's skin, was the perfect outline of my fingers. Small puffs of dark smoke came from his skin, and he was moaning. The shape of my hand slowly faded from view.

"What does this mean?" Kimiko asked.

I turned to face her. "Listen, you said that it takes twelve hours for the DNA of anyone infected to be rewritten, right?"

She nodded.

"It hasn't even been an hour since Harada was bitten. The virus hasn't had anywhere near the time it needs to finish its work."

The doctor just stared at me. "Where are you going with this?"

I felt the mask move as I grinned. "That means my DNA will not harm Harada."

Her eyes widened slightly as she registered this fact. The implications were huge.

"My question to you, Doctor, is this: can you inject those antigens that kill the virus into Harada?"

She shook her head. "I am sorry, Walt. I cannot

do this."

My heart sank. "Why not?"

She shrugged. "We never separated the antigens from your blood. There was no point. By the time we accomplish this, Harada will have changed. It is a good idea, but we cannot do this."

"A transfusion."

"What?"

I laughed. "Just give him my blood. The antigens will be in there. My DNA won't hurt him. You could burn the virus right out of him."

Her eyes bulged. "It is unlikely that you have the same blood type as Harada. There are serious risks and complications from using the wrong type for a patient."

I snorted a laugh. "Are any of them worse than death? Are any of them worse than being sentenced to becoming a vampire for life?"

"He could still die, Walt."

"He could live, Doctor."

She turned and walked up to the patient. Her hand went to Harada's forehead and lightly touched where my hand had been just a moment before.

I walked up beside her. "I think we should let Harada decide." She gave me a hard look.

"I'm serious! Tell him the risks and the possibilities, and let him decide. He deserves to know. Right now, I'm the best chance he's got."

The doctor walked over to a table and readied

a needle. She loaded it with a clear substance and then came back to Harada. After finding a vein and injecting the full syringe, she stepped back.

Harada's eyes fluttered, and he came to. The doctor greeted him and started talking. I didn't understand the words, as they were in Japanese, but the meaning was clear. She was laying it all out. Harada's eyes kept darting from her to me and back again.

When she finished, he beckoned me closer. He took my hand and said something in his language, then closed his eyes.

I looked at the doctor, and she translated for me. "He says it was an honor to fight with you, and he would rather die fighting the virus than becoming Kyūketsuki. He does not want to be a vampire for a moment in this life."

Ten minutes later, I was lying beside Harada. A couple of nurses and the doctor were getting ready to do a transfusion. Judging from the number of people setting up and helping, it looked to be a little more serious than I'd anticipated. What had I gotten myself into?

I cleared my throat to get the doctor's attention. "Uh, Doctor Kimiko, what happens when the wrong blood type is put into someone? I mean, what do they experience?"

She arched an eyebrow and gave me a look. "You have chosen an unusual time to ask this question, Walt."

I laughed. "Humor me."

"It is not pleasant. He will have brown urine, fever, chills, nausea, and some pain in parts of his body. In his weakened state, it may kill him."

"And if it doesn't?"

She let out a sigh. "If Harada does not perish, it should be interesting to see how the virus is affected."

"Sounds like we're doing some weird science here today," I said with a grimace.

The doctor put her hand on my shoulder. "We are doing the only thing we can do in this extraordinary situation." She got a needle ready while she kept talking to me. "Walt, you are not going to be awake for this procedure. I will be monitoring both of you during this event. I will keep you safe."

She pushed the needle into my arm, and I felt the ingredients heat up my vein. My vision started clouding, and the last thing I remembered before I went out was the man beside me starting to scream.

# CHAPTER 30

I came out of a deep sleep, some dream still at the edge of my mind. I looked around and was surprised to see I was in my room. The white box with the big television had become home. How did I get here? How long had I been out?

Pushing back the blankets, I stretched and yawned. My mouth was dry, and I still felt tired. Harada! I suddenly remembered what had put me in bed in the first place. Stepping out of bed, I wobbled and had to sit back on the mattress. Then, I grabbed my robe and slippers and made my way out the door.

Ito was standing there, and his eyes bulged when he saw me. "No, no! Walt san, rest," he said, marching toward me. It was a good suggestion.

I held up a hand of my own. "Harada?" I asked.

He shrugged. "Don't know. Walt san, rest!" he insisted again. "Breakfast?" he asked as I made my way back to bed.

"Ugh!" I groaned as I lay back down. "Breakfast in bed?"

"Hai."

I blinked a couple of times and thought about it. "Okay, steak and eggs?"

Ito nodded and stopped a nurse in the hallway. They had a brief conversation, and she went on her way. Then he bowed at me and closed my door.

I must have nodded off because I woke up when the door opened, and Ito was delivering my breakfast on a tray. Sure enough, steak and eggs were on the plate. "Harada?" I asked him again.

He shook his head. "Don't know, Walt san."

*Damn!* Still, I was starving, so I dug into the food, and it was excellent. I was feeling stronger by the minute. Still light-headed, but I didn't feel like I was going to fall anymore. I got up and started walking.

The people at the facility were staring again, but their eyes were wider. They weren't curious. They were looking at me with a new point of view. Why?

I got to the hospital wing and saw Kimiko. She saw me, too, and marched right up to me. "You should not be up. I will have Ito's head!"

"Relax!" I told her with a smile. "I woke up on my own and had breakfast. I'm fine." The smile ran away from my face. "Harada?"

She took a breath and let it out slowly. A smile slowly curved her lips. "Come and see for yourself." Kimiko walked me through the doors that led to the room with the big window. My eyes were wide, and I didn't blink as I walked up to Harada's bed.

And there he was. Alive! Lying in bed, eyes closed. His skin was still pale, and I could see his chest moving as he breathed. "Yes!" I yelped and then clamped a hand over my mouth. The doctor brought a hand to her lips to silence me. "How is he? I mean… did he change?"

She smiled as she whispered, "He did not. He did experience great pain during his recovery, and he still has to deal with the effects of receiving blood that was the wrong type."

"But he'll be okay?"

"We believe he will."

I did a silent cheer and pumped my fist in the air. "Way to go, Doc! That's great!"

The doctor folded her arms over her chest and raised her eyebrows. "It is much more than that. His body has rejected the virus, and he now carries the antigen needed to defeat the illness."

I grinned at her. "And he doesn't carry my DNA, am I right?"

"That is true," she said with a straight face.

My smile faltered. "So, isn't this a cure?"

She sighed. "Walt, it is a treatment for anyone recently bitten and infected."

"But not for anyone who has had their DNA rewritten a long time ago," I guessed, looking at the floor.

She came closer and put a hand on my arm. "I am sorry, Walt. Because of you and Harada, we believe we now have antigens to administer to someone before that takes place. It will do nothing for someone who has already undergone the transformation."

"Oh, well. I guess it's good news that you might have something to help someone who was just bitten."

"It is," she agreed with a nod. "Now, please return to your bed! Oyabun is coming to see you personally this evening. He wants you in good health, and he is not to be disappointed."

I was still aching from the disappointment of learning a cure was still out of reach. "Okay, I'll go rest. I don't want anyone getting in trouble." I turned and started walking away from her.

"Walt," she called softly. "He won't be alone. Representatives from America and Russia will be with him."

I stopped dead. "Foster? Kamenev?"

A nod.

"What would make them come all this way?"

She walked closer and spoke under her breath. "We have a great deal to show them, and I am told that there have been significant developments over the last twenty-four hours."

"The vampires?" I guessed.

"Yes. They know."

I frowned. "How much do they know?"

"They know everything, Walt."

# CHAPTER 31

Lying in my bed, looking at the ceiling, and letting my thoughts bounce around my skull was more time-consuming than I thought. Before I knew it, there was a knock at the door, and Oyabun walked in with a couple of tough-looking sentries. I swung my legs out of bed to get up and bow, but the old man held up both hands and told me to stop. "No, no! Stay in bed," he said.

I did as he asked—the guy is the leader of the Yakuza, so he gets what he wants. A second later, Kamenev walked in with a couple of his own heavies. "Mister Kamenev!" I cheered.

He smiled and walked right up to me. That warm handshake was delivered again. "Good to see you, Walt. This is becoming a habit."

"I don't mind this habit," I chuckled.

Agent Foster was just behind him with some guys who would fit right in on a professional football field. The cut of their suits and hair made it obvious they were from America. I suddenly remembered Elena telling me that it wasn't that hard to tell. She was right.

The older agent took my hand with a good grip and smiled. "A pleasure to meet you face to face. How are you feeling?"

"I'm fine. Good, actually."

Kamenev held up a hand. "You have one more person that needs to see you briefly." The crowd of security and representatives parted to let a small nurse push in a patient in a wheelchair.

"Harada!" I laughed. "Look at you!"

The Japanese fighter looked so much better than he had earlier. There was more color to his skin, and his eyes were alert. "Walt san, thank you." His voice was strong and clear. He rolled up to my bed and shook my hand with vigor.

"Hey, anytime. It's good to see you getting better, Harada."

"Hai," he said with a quick bow that I returned.

I looked around the room. "I'm feeling a little weird about being the only one in the room still in bed. Should I get up?"

The men in the room all gave a small snort of laughter and a polite smile. "Not at all," Kamenev answered. "We will ask all security personnel to leave so that we may meet quickly. There is much to discuss."

Without a word, the security detail for each

of these important men walked out into the hall, and as the door was about to close, Kimiko walked in. She wasn't wearing her lab coat but an elegant navy pantsuit. I noticed she was wearing more delicate glasses that really allowed her beautiful eyes to be appreciated. Her low heels made a slight click on the tiles as she walked in. "Ah, you are all here. Welcome!" she announced.

After greeting the doctor, Kamenev and Foster looked at each other. The American was the first to speak. "The vampire nation knows all about Walt and what he represents. They knew we had a way to kill them, but not the specifics. They didn't have all the facts."

"And now they do?" I guessed.

"Yes, they do," Foster confirmed. "They were reluctant to believe that it was a person that had this ability, but they have come to accept it, and they are not going quietly into that good night."

Kamenev sighed. "We have seen worldwide mobilization. Even more interesting is that secrecy is no longer their priority. There have been mistakes, and people are asking questions."

I blinked at him. "Are you telling me the world knows? I mean, really knows about these things?"

Foster held up a hand to slow me down. "Just a few incidents, but with everyone carrying a recording device these days, people are asking questions. Some of the videos cannot be explained away."

"There was a failed bid to gain information in Moscow," Kamenev said. "The fiends had bad intelligence and believed that the answers lay in the bottom of the building where you and I first met, Walt. They infiltrated but were ultimately dispatched by Russian special forces, Spetsnaz."

"Wow!" my eyes bugged out. "Is…is Svetlana okay?"

The Russian's eyes softened, and a smile eased onto his face. "Svetlana is fine, Walt. The things were only concerned about breaking into the basement. The only thing they found was death."

Foster cleared his throat. "It seems that they finally know where the threat is located. We have seen Japan and the South Alps come up a great deal in communication on the dark web and a great deal of mobilization."

"Vampires don't fly. They are too obvious on a plane, and they need to feed. As a result, boats and trains are moving like never before," Kamenev added. "And they're all going to one destination."

"Japan?" I guessed.

Foster and Kamenev looked at each other. "Yeah, Walt." Foster acknowledged. "They're coming to Japan."

Kamenev held up a finger. "There are also reports of a revolution of sorts in the vampire society."

Everyone in the room looked at him. "What kind of revolution?" Kimiko asked.

"The younger members, the ones recently turned, are looking to change their fortunes. They see no future in fighting the rest of the world. They are seeking asylum or a cure of some kind."

Foster shook his head, looking down. "The old guard won't like that. They won't like that one bit!"

"Nyet," Kamenev agreed. "They do not."

"Which brings us to our visit," Foster said, putting his hands in his pockets. "The younger vampires believe we have weaponry that can't be beat. We're here to see it in action."

"Very well," Kimiko spoke up. "If you gentlemen will follow me, I will take you to the fourth level, and you will be shown what we have learned." She looked at me. "Walt, are you sure you want to see this?"

I took a breath and let it out slowly. "Yeah, I think I need to know."

# CHAPTER 32

The fourth sublevel was much brighter than I remembered. A few more lights were on and there were four cells that were completely empty. I'd destroyed those test subjects. Totally self-defense, and nothing I could do...but that didn't mean I had to like it.

"Subject number six," Kimiko announced as we got to the cell. "This is a male vampire captured in Sicily. He is approximately eighty years old." The lights went on in the cell, and a tall, greasy-haired creature in a hospital gown stood up and hissed. Its dark eyes were pure malevolence as it glared at us.

The doctor looked at a clipboard that was on a plastic shelf outside the cell. "This one took twenty bullets and kept coming. It was finally stunned by a construction worker smashing its skull with a sledgehammer." She put down the clipboard and regarded us. "Because he had just fed, he made a full recovery after being captured." She looked over at Ito and nodded.

The Yakuza moved closer to the door, took out his automatic pistol, and released the magazine. He passed it to the Oyabun with a bow. The older Japanese man took it, inspected the ammunition, and passed it to Kamenev. I held up my hand to refuse when it was offered to me, so the Russian gave it back to Ito.

"The bullets are a hard acrylic that are able to pierce the skin, and then they release their center into the target." She looked at me. "The center is made up of a liquid that contains Walt's DNA that we have synthesized. It is most effective."

"May we see it in action?" Foster asked. I knew someone would.

Oyabun nodded at Ito, and he returned the gesture. He slid the magazine back in the pistol, chambered a round, and opened the door to cell number six. The occupant reached for the man as he shot him. The creature reared back, eyes huge and clutching at its chest. In a heartbeat, a hole the size of a cannonball opened in the center of the vampire, and it collapsed to the ground. The body sizzled and oozed in all directions.

"Most effective," Kamenev said with a smile. "One of these new bullets succeeded when twenty regular bullets failed. When can these be made available to our forces?"

Doctor Kimiko smiled. "Your teams are being provided with this unique ammunition at this very moment. We are very confident it will be devastating."

She walked over to a cell a little further down the hall and grabbed the clipboard on the shelf just outside the door. She turned a few pages and looked up at us. "This will be a different experiment. It is using the plasma that recent events have produced." She looked at me. "I'm sure you're aware of the transfusion that Mister Baranov provided Harada to help him counteract the infection."

"Hai," Oyabun said and gave me a solemn nod. I returned it because I didn't know what else to do. Kamenev just smiled.

"This is a female subject who is roughly two hundred years in age." She put down the clipboard and sighed. "She was captured in France. She had just fed on two infants in a nursery. The father buried a fire poker in her head, and that was enough to stun her." She turned the lights on in the cell.

A small, scrawny woman with lank brown hair hanging on her face rose from the ground. You could see her ribs through the hospital gown. I couldn't see her eyes, but her teeth were on display. I wished they weren't. A collection of misshapen fangs and broken incisors ringed her black mouth, and a dark tongue lolled out from her lips. A high-pitched scream escaped that emaciated body.

The doctor pointed to the ceiling, and a moment later, a bag of blood dropped out of the slot to land at the creature's feet. It dropped to all fours and gorged itself on the contents. Disgusting sucking sounds and slurping could be heard outside the cell. The noise stopped, and the thing stood up tall. It threw its head back and screamed again, spreading its arms wide like it was on a cross. Suddenly, it fell on its back and just continued to scream.

"Walt's DNA is not in the creature, but the antigens from Harada are making their way through her body. The virus is being destroyed slowly, and the cells that were rewritten so long ago are returning to what they were." She looked at me and sighed. "Sadly, the cells do not survive this regression, and death is slow and quite painful. This is most likely because the cells have been in their present state for so long."

Kimiko started walking down the hall. Inside, I was screaming because she was getting closer and closer to cell number twenty. She wouldn't experiment on Irina right in front of Kamenev, would she?

She found a clipboard at cell seventeen, and I began to breathe easier. The occupant of this cell was the little Japanese man with the ponytail. The very one who had released the vampires in the hope of killing both me and Harada. He had a wound on his neck that was oozing blood. I glared at the little creep, and he gave it right back with wild eyes until he saw Oyabun. Then he looked at the ground and swallowed. Yeah, he knew it was over.

"This is a most unexpected finding," the doctor said as she looked at the clipboard. "The subject was infected about two hours ago. He was then given Harada's antigens. With minimal discomfort, he completely recovered from the initial infection."

"You have a way to counteract the virus before it finishes altering the victim?" Kamenev asked.

"Yes," the doctor said with a nod. "If we can get to someone before the virus has completely rewritten the DNA of the infected, we can expect a full recovery." She brought her hand to her chin. "We do not know how far a victim can change and for how long before Harada's antigens are no longer effective. It does appear that the duration affects the pain the subject experiences. The longer infected, the greater the agony."

Oyabun said something in Japanese to Kimiko, and she nodded. He looked at Ito, and the Yakuza soldier immediately opened the door and put a round right between the eyes of the little man. He dropped and twitched on the floor.

I'd just watched them murder a man! *Yakuza*... you didn't mess with them, and it didn't look like they tolerated any betrayal. I don't know what the vampires paid the little man, but I hoped his family got to keep it, and I hoped it was a lot.

"That concludes our demonstration today," the doctor explained. "There is one more thing that we would like to do." She looked at me. "Walt, Oyabun has a gift for you."

"A gift?"

The doctor walked closer and looked up at me. "Yes. It is a weapon that is only for you. It is a great honor."

I looked at the scary old gangster and bowed. He returned it smartly, a small smile on his lips.

The doctor touched my arm and pointed at my Russian friend. "You should thank Mister Kamenev as well. His input was invaluable in the design of this weapon."

I looked at Kamenev and smiled. He shrugged. "Think of it as a Russian weapon with a Japanese design."

"Sounds intriguing," I said with a chuckle.

"It is waiting for you in your room," Doctor Kimiko said. "Follow me, gentlemen, and we will present Mister Baranov with his gift." She turned and walked away, with Oyabun right behind her and Kamenev following as well.

After a couple of steps, I looked back over my shoulder at cell twenty. I could see Irina standing, leaning her forehead against the glass. One hand was up, pressed on the window, waiting for mine.

# CHAPTER 33

"Open it," Kamenev said with a grin. Oyabun was standing beside him with his hands clasped behind his back. Doctor Kimiko was watching with a bemused look on her face.

A long black case was on my bed. I guessed someone dropped it off while we were watching experimental murder on the fourth floor.

I shrugged, threw the catches on the side that was closest, and opened the case. I'd seen weapons like this in old history books. It had a long, thin, round shaft that ended in a ball covered in spikes. The words *Medusa's Son* were engraved on one side, and there were many other languages etched into the head of this club. It was right out of medieval times.

This one had some modern aspects, though. The handle was black and looked like graphite. There was a strap on the handle so it wouldn't be lost. A red button was on the top of the handle. "Wow! It's amazing, but what is it, and how does it work?" I asked.

Kamenev laughed. "It is a slightly larger version of something called a morning star. This one is different. When you press the button, three small needles come out of the handle to pierce the skin and draw blood to the tip of each spike. The batteries that power it are good for decades. When this is in your hand, it is deadly to the vampires of the world."

I took it out of the case and hefted it in my right hand. It was lighter than I expected. My thumb crept toward the button, but Kamenev put a hand on my arm. "Make sure it is in your left hand when you press that button. It may inhibit your ability to use the weapon if your palm is lacerated."

Oyabun stepped forward. "We considered a sword, a Japanese Katana."

I laughed. "I think it's more likely that I'd hurt myself with that big blade."

Everyone in the room smiled. "That was our conclusion as well," the doctor explained. "This seemed like the easiest weapon for a person without training to use on those infected with the virus."

I moved it to my left hand and pressed the button. Sure enough, I felt a sharp stab in my palm. "Ow!" After a moment, I shifted it over to my right hand. I saw blood drops at the end of each of the spikes. It was a menacing weapon before, and now it was dripping with my DNA. Looking at my left, I could see three small wounds in the palm of my hand.

I got a tissue and dried the tips as I spoke. "Oyabun, Mister Kamenev, this is a great honor. Thank you so much." I placed it back in the case.

The two men nodded their acknowledgement, and the doctor spoke up. "I need some time with my patient, please, gentlemen. Would you excuse us?"

"Of course, Doctor Kimiko. Keep our young friend healthy," Kamenev said. He shook my hand and left with Oyabun.

The attractive doctor looked my way when they left. "Please sit on the bed while I check your vitals."

I did as she asked. "Hey, Doc, thanks for not selecting number twenty down there."

She smiled as she put the inflatable sleeve on my arm to check my blood pressure. "I made a promise. I mean to keep it."

"Still, I'm grateful."

Kimiko finished checking me over and looked at her watch. "It's almost feeding time on the fourth level. Isn't there somewhere you would rather be?"

I smiled at her. "Thanks, Doctor Kimiko." I got off the bed and hurried across the room.

My hand was on the doorknob when the doctor spoke up. "Walt." I turned to see her tapping on her elegant watch with a frown. "She doesn't have much time."

*** 

I went to the glass on Irina's cell and looked up at the ceiling. Sure enough, a bell rang, and three bags of blood fell to the tile floor. Irina left her usual hiding spot under the bunk and attacked her meal. I could hear her slurping up the liquid, even going so far as to lap it off the tiles. She needed it.

My hand went up to the glass, and I waited. A moment later, she was there, and her hand went up to mirror mine on the glass. "*Syn meduzy, Walt,*" she cried softly. "*It is you?*"

I couldn't lie to her. Not now. "Yes, Irina. I don't want to be. Something in me is bad for...people like you."

"*Eto konets. It is the end.*" She wailed, and tears of blood left the corners of her eyes. Still, she didn't move her hand from mine.

"Would that be so bad, Irina? Do you really want to live like this?"

She took a deep breath, and I heard it rasp out of her slight body. Her haunting voice came back. "*Da... want to live. Want talk with Walt.*"

I felt my eyes tear up, and my throat closed. It was hard to speak. "I want that too, Irina. I want that, too."

# CHAPTER 34

I made my way to the hospital wing of the facility. Took some time, but I found the private room that held Harada. As soon as I walked in, my old friend tried to get out of his chair to greet me. "No, no!" I said with a chuckle, holding both hands up. "Harada san, you must not stand up."

The tough Yakuza heavy ignored me and stood anyway. He wobbled, then bowed deep. I knew enough to bow quickly and straighten up to release him.

He held out a hand, and I shook it. "Thank you, Walt san." His accent was heavy, but the look in his eyes said more than his words.

"You fought for me down there. I just did the same."

"Walt, you save life."

I smiled at the man. "A life worth saving." A small Japanese nurse came in and smiled at me. She was wearing a surgical mask and hat, but her eyes conveyed her pleasant demeanor. I got an idea and spoke to the nurse. "Pardon, do you speak English?"

Her eyes wrinkled as she smiled, and she nodded. "I do."

I pointed to Harada, who had returned to his seat. "I need to talk to my friend, and my Japanese is very poor. Could you translate what I am saying in English for this good man?"

She bowed deeply. "Hai! It would be an honor."

"Dōmo arigatō," I replied with a bow. That was the extent of my Japanese. I looked at Harada. "My friend, I have to ask you to do something. Something important. You are the only one who can do this favor for me."

The small nurse spoke without emotion and translated for me. Harada listened and nodded. He frowned and looked at me. He spoke to the nurse, but his eyes rested on me. She turned my way. "He is loyal to the Yakuza and cannot violate his oath."

I held up a hand. "I would never ask you to betray the Yakuza, Harada san. What I ask will not affect the interests of Oyabun or the Yakuza. I am grateful to them for protecting me as they studied me."

The nurse spoke for a time, and Harada's frown left his face. He said a few words, and the nurse looked my way. "He says to go on. Ask your favor."

I smiled and put my hands in my pockets. "I am aware that the Yakuza and the Russians will sell the weapons they create from my blood to the highest bidder." I paused while the nurse spoke my words to the man in the chair. I could see both open their eyes a little wider.

"I am fine with this," I continued. "It is the way of the world that people will do what they must and seek profit where they can. The vampires are done, and the people who protected me and have lost so much deserve good fortune."

The nurse smiled with relief and translated. Harada was nodding as she spoke, and a small smile crept onto his face.

"As I say, I have a favor to ask, and you are the only one who can do this for me. I have asked for nothing, but I do ask for this."

The nurse translated for him. Harada looked me right in the eyes and nodded. "Hai, Walt san. Harada will do favor."

I wanted to dance around the room like a fool, but I held my emotions in check. "Good, good! I will explain what needs to be done."

After talking for a good five minutes about what I needed him to do and when he and the nurse looked at each other, she started speaking quickly to the man, but he silenced her with a wave of his hand. He stood up and looked at the nurse, who backed away, cowed by his anger. He held out a hand, and we shook. "It will be done," he said solemnly.

"I knew you wouldn't let me down. Thank you so much, Harada."

He bowed, and I returned it. "I must rest for coming battle, Walt. They come."

I nodded my head, thanked the nurse, and left Harada to his recovery. He was absolutely right. The entire rage and fear of the vampire nation was about to come crashing down on the facility. The battle would be fought and won in the South Alps of Japan. For the first time since I'd arrived, I had trouble sleeping.

# CHAPTER 35

The alarm rang quietly, and I woke up. Didn't feel too refreshed, so I guess the quality of sleep wasn't that good. All things considered, that was to be expected. I used the bathroom and staggered back to the bed. I put on the robe and stretched. Time to get moving.

I opened the door and started down the hall, yawning again. I saw soldiers dressed in black carrying automatic weapons marching the other way. A couple looked at me sideways, as I wasn't dressed like anyone else. I looked like a guy walking to the end of the driveway to get the newspaper.

A moment later, another platoon of soldiers marched by. There was no mistaking the American flag on their camo uniforms. Definitely some of Foster's men. One gave me a wink as they hustled by. "USA!" I called at their back and got a thumbs-up from a couple of them who didn't look back.

I was almost at the cafeteria when I saw a

completely different squad of soldiers dressed in immaculate suits and sunglasses and radiating ferocity. The Yakuza were on the move. I stopped walking and bowed low, smiling.

The Yakuza froze and returned the bow, releasing me. They nodded at me as they passed, and I returned the gesture. I didn't know if they were on patrol or taking their positions. The only thing I knew for sure was that they were getting ready. We all were.

Steak and eggs for breakfast. Why not! This was going to be my last breakfast at this madhouse, no matter what happened next. I asked the guy taking my order for the biggest steak he had and three eggs, over easy. He smiled, and I doubted he took me seriously. I was wrong.

The plate that he handed over had a steak that looked about the size of a frisbee, lightly browned toast, and three eggs cooked to perfection. I just started laughing when I saw it, and so did the guy behind the counter. Looks like I wasn't the only one celebrating.

I grabbed a coffee and cutlery and found a table. The steak cut like butter and tasted heavenly! The eggs were just as good. This helped. Focusing on a breakfast for a king was probably one of the best things to happen to me since I arrived. Another one of the benefits of this place walked up when I was almost finished.

Doctor Kimiko came to the table, pulled out a chair, and sat. She wasn't wearing her lab coat but jeans and a sweatshirt. "Good morning, Walt."

I was just shoveling a piece of yolk-covered steak into my mouth, but I let the fork drop down to the plate. "Oh, hey! Doctor Kimiko, you look...different."

She smiled. "My duties are different today."

"How so?" I asked, and shoved the steak into my mouth.

The doctor shrugged. "Research is on hold for now. I am supervising the movement of what we have discovered and what we have created."

I finished chewing and took a swig of my coffee. "How's that going?"

"Almost finished," she said, leaning forward and putting her elbows on the table. "Everything is being moved to the roof for transportation."

"Helicopter?" I guessed.

She nodded. "Yes. It is vital that the samples and research leave this facility and are shared with the world."

"For a price," I said with a wink.

Her smile vanished. "What are you saying?"

"Oh, come on, Doctor. We both know it's going to be sold. There's nothing wrong with that. The Yakuza and Russians put a lot of capital into this place and the work you've done. Only fair if they get some of it back or a profit."

She tilted her head to one side and smirked at me. "And you aren't asking for any money yourself?"

I shrugged. "Just do me a favor and don't hit the Americans too hard. That seems like the nicest thing to do."

"I will never understand the way your mind works, Walt."

I laughed. "Sometimes I don't understand myself."

She laughed, too, and held up a hand. "I'm here to talk to you about how you will leave this facility."

"My time is up?"

"Yes, it is time you packed your belongings. When the guards finish their sweep and the path is declared safe, you will be part of a convoy that takes you to the airport."

I sat back in the chair. "Well, most of my things are still in my bag. You gave me clothing and toiletries. I can be ready in about ten minutes."

She held up a finger. "You have much longer than that. The focus is to get the research out. A few employees are leaving in a convoy first. You and the research team go last."

"So, how long are we talking here?"

Kimiko looked at the table. "You will probably just finish lunch and then be on the move."

A terrible thought ran through my mind. "You're not moving the test subjects, are you?"

She wouldn't look me in the eyes. "No."

"What are you doing with the test subjects, Doctor?" I asked in a whisper.

"I am to destroy them," she said with a sigh. "I cannot save subject twenty. I am sorry, Walt."

I stood up and looked down. "Her name is Irina."

"Walt, I tried."

I sighed and looked at my slippers. "Can I ask you for one thing?"

"Yes."

"Please make ending her the very last thing you do. Can you do that, Doctor Kimiko?" When I looked at her, I was surprised to see tears in her eyes.

"Yes, Walt. I promise."

I felt my own eyes get blurry. "Thanks. I guess it's time to say goodbye."

# CHAPTER 36

The walk from the cafeteria to my room was a blur. I didn't see many people, and they weren't seeing me. The novelty was gone, and everyone was moving on. So why couldn't I?

I got to my room, walked in, and just stood there. I looked around, taking it all in. I saw the suitcase that was sent with me from Russia and walked over to retrieve it. The bag was packed and ready to go in two minutes flat. I even managed to cram in a few souvenirs. The slippers and robe were definitely keepers, and I liked the soap they gave me. I stole a few bars. The shampoo sucked. They could keep that.

The bed was unmade, so I walked over and started straightening out the sheets. When my hand went under my pillow, I felt something soft, something that was not a pillow. I froze. I lifted the pillow fast, and it was there. I laughed and smiled. "Harada, you are the best!" I whispered to myself.

I put the pillow back fast, concealing Harada's gift, and laid down on the bed. My eyes were open as I mulled it all over. Timing was going to be everything, and I had to be very careful not to let anyone know what I was doing. I had no way of knowing if I would be stopped or what else might happen.

The doctor said I would be leaving after lunch. That was cutting it close. I was pretty sure I could get where I needed to be and make my way to the cafeteria with nobody the wiser. I took a deep breath and let it out. I was lying to myself. There was so much that could go wrong, and there was always the unexpected. Still, I had to try.

I thought of Irina and the other test subjects deep in the fourth sublevel. It was incredible that their lives would be over in hours. They didn't know, and even if someone explained it, they were so far out of their minds with hunger that they probably wouldn't have understood.

See, that was the one thing that kept bothering me. The contradiction that kept coming up again and again. The vampires were supposed to be mindless, raging monsters. I knew what they meant. I'd seen it. Even in Irina, I'd seen it!

But there was something else. Something I'd seen and heard. When they were fed, when they were full, they were rational. They had a memory, even a sense of humor. The doctor said they couldn't make their own blood cells. That's why they fed on others.

Was it that desperate need that fueled their madness?

My thoughts were interrupted by a knock, and Doctor Kimiko came in. Her eyes were wide, and she wasn't smiling. "Walt, I need to tell you something."

Still laying on the bed, I got up on one elbow. "What's the matter, Doc?"

The doctor took a couple of steps to be closer. "The first convoy didn't make it."

I swung my legs over the bed and looked up at her. "What do you mean, 'didn't make it?'"

She folded her arms over her chest, not defensively, but like she was hugging herself. "It was ambushed on the long road through the Alps. The drivers and the passengers are dead. Every one of them."

I stood up. "Oh my God!"

The doctor did something I would never have expected. She started to cry. Then it hit me. She probably knew every single person that died. Probably interviewed and hired every one of the researchers.

I didn't see her as a doctor or the head of a big research project. I didn't even see her as the granddaughter of a Yakuza boss. I saw her as my friend, and I moved to hug her. She let me.

I asked the only question I could. "What happened to them?"

She sniffed back some tears and explained. "The convoy was hit about an hour after they left. Vampires with weapons shot the drivers. They pulled the rest from their cars and fed. They fed…" She was unable to continue.

"I'm so sorry," I said. What else was there to say?

Her hands went to my shoulders, and she broke our embrace. "Walt, we have to change our plans. We cannot risk another convoy. The helicopter picked up the first half of our research and samples. When it returns, we must send everyone who can fit on the helicopter out of harm's way." She wiped her eyes and gave me a hard look. "You need to be on that helicopter."

I shook my head. "No, that's okay. I'll catch the next one."

"Walt, you must survive!"

"Doctor, I'm the one who has the least to fear from these things. I should be the last person to get out of here."

"They have guns, Walt."

I laughed. "And so do Harada, Ito, and the rest of the Yakuza. I'll join them. Protect them, and protect you. I can do more good that way. You have what you need from me."

"I do not like it. But…I see your logic." She took a breath and sighed. "Grab your things and make your way to the hospital wing. The helipad is on the roof."

"Sure thing, Doc. I'll be right behind you."

She hung her head and turned to leave. "Do not delay, Walt. The attack on the facility could happen at any moment."

"Right behind you, I swear."

She nodded and left. The second I heard the door close, I ran to the bed, stuffed Harada's gift into a pillowcase, and looked around the room. I walked up to the black case, threw the latches, and opened it. I easily hefted the engraved mace in my hand and ran to the door. "Just have to throw up a Hail Mary first, Doctor."

# CHAPTER 37

I ran down the hallway, and a couple of terrified-looking researchers still in their lab coats were running in the opposite direction. "You're going the wrong way!" one of them called at my back.

"Be there in a minute," I lied, and kept running. When I got to the escalators, I didn't wait for them to do their job. I ran down the stairs, getting lower and lower into the facility. Damn it! This was happening too fast. I could work the first part of my plan, but that was all. It would have to do.

I got to the fourth level and ran around looking for an office or a control center. Took a moment, but I found a door that looked promising. It was locked, so I lifted the mace and swung it hard at the handle. The handle broke off, and I jimmied the lock to open it up. Bingo! Bags of blood were there, as were the automatic releases for the doors of the test subjects.

Looking them over, I set down the mace, put on

some rubber gloves, and picked up the three largest blood bags. Making my way to cell number twenty, I put my hand against the glass and spoke into the intercom. "Irina? It's Walt."

There was no waiting this time. I saw her small, pale, and filthy hand come out from under the bunk. She was wearing the blanket like a sarong over her soiled hospital gown. She staggered up to the glass, and her hand mirrored mine. Her forehead leaned against the glass, and I heard her voice rasp through the intercom. *"Walt...talk to Walt."*

I smiled, and my heart raced. She couldn't know what was going to happen next. Truth was, neither did I. But it was everything. "Yes, Irina. Yes, we can talk. But I need to feed you first. You need to be strong."

Two steps to my left, and I was standing at the slot at the door. It was tricky with the rubber gloves, and I could feel my hands sweating with the heat and my nerves. I shoveled the three bags of blood into Irina's cell, one at a time. The first bag had barely hit the ground before she was savaging it and feeding with abandon.

I walked back to the small window and watched her hunched over her meal. I was hoping that she would take her time. I wasn't looking forward to what was coming next. Was this going to be her last meal?

She stood up, arched her back in a stretch, and let out a low moan. She walked back to the window and put her hand on the glass. *"Walt feed Irina? Why?"*

I put my hand on hers on my side of the glass and took a shuddering breath, trying to compose myself. I didn't want to cry. I didn't want her to be afraid. At the end of her life, I only wanted her to feel wanted. "Irina, you are right. I fed you because I want you to have a chance. I must do something I do not want to do. I don't know what is going to happen, but I have to try."

Her pale hand wiped some blood off her chin while her dark eyes looked into my soul. "*Feel better... feel strong!*" she said.

"Good, that's good," I said, my voice breaking. "I have more for you, but this one is different. It's your only chance, Irina." I looked at the floor, and I couldn't stop the tears. I looked back at her unblinking eyes. "I'm sorry. There's no time for anything else. It was all I could do to get this one chance."

"*Okay, Walt. I am hungry. You have more?*"

I nodded and dug into the pillowcase. I found the bag filled with Harada's blood and slipped it through the door. I heard Irina hit the bag and start to feed. Again, I walked over to the window and peeled off my rubber gloves to see what would happen next.

To my surprise, Irina finished the entire bag. She stood up again and looked my way. And then it happened. She started to blink rapidly and then screamed as she collapsed on the floor. I turned and ran to the control room. I heard a shout from the floor above me. Damn it! Too soon!

With the vampires attacking from outside the facility, it would be too dangerous to have any that could attack us from within. Not safe for anyone in the facility, and it might not be safe for Irina. But there was no way to know. I had planned on staying with her, but that was impossible now.

I pressed the buttons that released every test subject on the fourth sub-level and hefted the morning star into my left hand. My thumb pressed the button, and I winced as I felt the three needles puncture my palm. I moved the weapon back to my right hand and walked out of the control room.

I could hear hissing and movement on the fourth sub-floor. I smiled and called out, "Come on, fellas, I'm right here. Dinner is served!"

# CHAPTER 38

They came running around the corner, full tilt. Greasy hair plastered to their scalps, eyes bulging, and arms reaching out of their flimsy hospital gowns. Bare feet slapped the smooth tiles on the floor. Their mouths were wide open, drooling, and tongues lolling out.

I almost laughed. I swung the mace in a wide arc, and droplets of my blood sprayed through the air at the gang of vampires. The first three dropped like stones, clutching whatever part of their body had absorbed the blood spatter.

I brought the mace back along the same arc with a backhanded swing that released some more blood. That took down the next two vampires, leaving one. One more monster to crush. It had to die so everyone else could live. There was no other way.

The thing was tall and very skinny. Its hands were huge, as was its mouth. It shrieked as it reached for me, but I had already wound up. It was fast, but not fast enough. I was bringing the mace from low to high like a golf swing.

I felt the impact as the head of the morning star caught the creature right under the jaw. It knocked the head back, and the vampire toppled over. I stood over the thing as it thrashed around, and the skull collapsed, turning into a bloody mess.

I could hear Irina screaming from her cell, and I took a step to check on her, but then I realized...what could I really do? There was no way to know what Harada's blood was doing to her. It was a sure bet that the virus was being destroyed, but what was it doing to her DNA? I couldn't comfort her or hold her in any way. If my skin touched any cells of hers that were still rewritten by the virus, it would start a chemical reaction that would be catastrophic. As it turned out, the choice was made for me.

Harada and Ito came running down the escalator into the fourth sublevel, dressed in suits, guns drawn. Obviously, they were looking for me. They looked around at the vampires on the ground, writhing as they dissolved and died. Harada pointed at me. "Walt! Come now!"

We all turned as we heard a scream from the floor above. It sounded close. I ran past them up the escalator. "Try to keep up, guys!" I shouted as I ran by them. I could hear their footfalls on the escalator behind me as we sprinted up to the next level.

We came upon a couple of vampires dressed in

blue hazmat suits that completely covered them. They were pinning a young woman on the ground, and she was thrashing for all she was worth.

The blue suits took away any doubt that they really did know about me. Well, not all about me. I buried the mace in the head of one of the vampires, and I felt the skull completely give way as I crushed it. The spikes must have pierced the skin of the suit because it died fast.

Harada tackled the remaining monster, and Ito emptied his gun into its head. I walked up and put my bloody left hand right on its face. It screamed and started choking on blood as it perished.

We turned to the woman they were attacking. It was Kimiko! She was being helped up by Harada. I found her glasses on the ground and picked them up. They seemed unharmed.

She was dazed and leaning on the Yakuza soldier for support. She had a hand on her neck, and blood oozed between her fingers. She'd been bitten. "Oh no," she whispered.

I grabbed her shoulders and made her look at me. "The medicine you made from Harada's blood, you need it!"

"The roof," she gasped. "It's all on the roof."

I looked at Harada, and something unspoken went between us. He helped the doctor walk while Ito and I took the lead. Good thing we did.

Three American soldiers came around the

corner, emptying their guns at something out of our field of view. They didn't even notice us.

Ito fell back to support Kimiko, and Harada came up on my left. He took out a magazine of the acrylic bullets filled with my blood, rammed it into the automatic pistol in his hand, and looked at me.

I shifted the mace to my left hand, and my thumb pressed the button. I winced and passed the weapon to my strong hand.

"Good," Harada grunted, and we both marched into the fray. "Right behind you!" I shouted to the soldiers as we came up behind them. "Fall back, guys. We got this."

We stepped past them to see what they were fighting. They had done a good job as a dozen vampires were writhing on the ground, full of bullets...but not dying. They were crawling towards their prey.

I swung the mace wide, and the crimson spatter started melting the faces of the four closest monsters. Harada squeezed a bullet into the head of the next three vampires behind them.

Stepping over the dissolving bodies of Harada's targets, I swung again. Same result. Three more dissolving vampires.

Harada shot one of the two remaining vampires, and I walked up to the last monster squirming on the floor. I put my foot on this throat and slapped my bloody palm on its forehead. It screamed for only a second before melting.

The soldiers stood there, guns pointed at the ground and their eyes wide. One of them with dark skin laughed. "You must be Baranov."

I winked at him. "What gave me away?"

All the soldiers started smiling and looking at each other. The one who spoke walked up to me and held out a hand. "Tyler Shaw, Green Beret."

I shook his hand. "Walt Baranov, freak of nature. I think you guys did a great job here."

Ito brought the doctor close. She didn't look good. "Roof!" he reminded us.

Looking at Shaw, I filled him in. "There's some medicine waiting on the roof of this place. She needs it, but I'm hoping there's enough for all of you to get a shot."

Shaw's dark eyes narrowed at me. "Why? What's in it?"

"Immunity from the virus that makes these things like this!"

He looked back at his team, and it was clear from the look on their faces that they were all for it. Time to get moving.

Harada and I took point. I stole a look back at Shaw. "These things we killed were ancient. Have all the vampires you've fought looked like that?"

"Yeah, come to think of it."

"That's the only good news I've heard today."

He frowned. "What? That they're old?"

I smirked at the soldier. "It's been said the

younger vampires are seeking some kind of amnesty. If we're seeing nothing but oldies, there could be some truth to it."

Shaw nodded his head. "Be nice if we didn't have to fight the entire vampire nation."

"You got that right," I laughed.

# CHAPTER 39

We got to the hospital wing, and the doctor spoke to Ito in Japanese. He said something to Harada, who led us to a stairway. It went up to a door and the roof. Harada went first, followed by Ito and the doctor. The soldiers went next, and I covered our backs.

I blinked in the sunlight when I got to the roof. It was a wide-open space, and we were standing about twenty feet from a helipad. There were about a dozen crates just off to the side, waiting for pickup. How far out was the helicopter? No way to know.

Ito and Harada helped the doctor over to the boxes, and the three of them started opening the packages and rifling through the contents. Kimiko found what she was looking for and prepared a shot. There was a small argument, and I think it was the doctor wanting to give others the shot first. Harada and Ito weren't having it, and they were right. She was too important, and that made her the priority. She gave in and administered the dose.

It was alarming when she dropped to her knees and cried out in pain. The two Yakuza heavies reached to help her, but she held up one hand to stop them, and the other went to her head. I don't understand Japanese, but it seemed like she was reassuring them that she would be okay. She got up on shaky legs and started looking for more equipment. When she found what she wanted, she beckoned the soldiers to come to her.

I looked around the facility. It was an amazing view. The small, rocky-tipped mountains that made up the Southern Alps of Japan were breathtaking in the sunlight. There was the lightest of breezes, and I could hear some birds singing unfamiliar songs.

The peace of nature was broken by the sound of gunfire and screams. I ran to the helipad to get a better view. Russian forces were in the forest, dressed in black and exchanging gunfire with a group of vampires. Some of them wore the same weird, blue hazmat suits. I figured that the creatures with guns were attacking at long range, and the ones decked out in the blue gear were meant for close-quarters fighting. It also showed that they knew all about me.

"Heads up!" I heard Shaw shout, and he was pointing to a distant corner of the roof. We could barely make out the creatures as they popped onto the roof one at a time. They must have formed a human ladder on the outside of the facility to allow them to get to higher ground and attack. They were determined. You had to give them that.

The three Green Beret warriors opened fire and hit two of the vampires, staggering them. Impressive as their aim was, they had only slowed them down. Ito and Harada each carried a box to the soldiers and got their attention. Harada pulled out an automatic pistol and offered it to Shaw. In answer, he pointed to his rifle and shook his head.

I walked closer to him. "Take the pistol, Shaw. Your rifle might be the better weapon, but you're going to love the ammunition in that gun."

Harada set down the box he was holding, aimed the pistol, and shot. He missed his first attempt, but the second hit the closest creature in the center of the chest. It dropped and screamed as it started to come apart.

Shaw grinned and looked at the other soldiers. "Switch 'em up, gentlemen!" They ran over, and each grabbed a pistol and a couple of magazines. "What's in these things?" Shaw asked as he destroyed a couple of vampires with as many shots as possible.

"Me," I answered. "They're acrylic bullets, and they've got samples of my blood in the center of them."

"Damn," he muttered as he dropped three more vampires. "You really are bad news for these things."

Even with the pistols and the excellent marksmanship of our team, it was getting harder and harder to keep the vampires at a distance. They were stepping over the bodies of the fallen creatures to get to us.

A low sound echoed down to us. "Helicopter!" Harada shouted and pointed in the distance. He had good eyes, as the thing was just a speck on the horizon. I looked from the aircraft in the distance to the danger in front of us. They were getting more and more numerous and closer.

I ran to the boxes and found a few more magazines. I brought them to the soldiers and the two Yakuza. I noticed they were taking very careful aim, not wanting to waste a single bullet. We would need every one of them.

The doctor was sitting on the ground near the boxes and hugging herself as she winced with pain. I ran over and took a knee beside her. "Doctor Kimiko, are you okay?"

She held up a hand. "I will be when the virus has been defeated. It is quite a painful process."

"Where does it hurt?"

"Everywhere," she cried, and gritted her teeth.

I looked up to see the vampires were still coming, and they were almost on top of us. Maybe it was my imagination, but each wave seemed to be older and more disgusting. Some were missing eyes or ears, and some were even crawling on the ground.

The mace was in my right hand, and I moved my thumb up to the button. This was going to hurt, and it wasn't recommended, but none of that mattered. I depressed the button and felt the needles pierce deep, draw blood, and retract. I felt the handle get sticky with blood. That would only help.

I stepped up and walked until I was near the line of shooters, careful not to step in front of them. I set myself with my left leg forward, empty hand outstretched, and the morning star out behind me. It was just a matter of time.

When I saw a filthy hand reach out and grab Ito's gun, I acted. I swung the mace and connected with the wide-open mouth of the vampire, and it fell back into the crowd, dying. I trotted over to Shaw and took out his knife. He gave me a sideways look that turned into a grim smile when he saw what I was doing. I smeared blood on the knife with my palm and handed it to him as he continued to shoot one-handed. I did the same for the other two soldiers and went back to protect Kimiko. She was looking a little better, but not much.

The helicopter was above us but hovering. I looked at the helipad, and all I saw were vampires lining up for their shot at the people alive on the roof. The helicopter couldn't land! I ran to Harada and pointed up. "Get the packages and the doctor out of here!"

I ran back to the door that gave us access to the facility and looked back. Sure enough, the vampires changed course and came right at me. The Green Beret soldiers continued to fire, but the important thing was that the helipad was clear. Shaw looked up at the aircraft and beckoned for the thing to land. Was it enough to save my friends? It was now or never.

# CHAPTER 40

I was swinging the mace back and forth wildly and backing up. The vampires were growling and snarling, drool falling from their fangs and open mouths. Yellowish eyes glared at me, but despite their fury, they were tentative in their attacks. They would feint with their hands and then fall back into each other. They knew who I was and what I could do. There was no doubt they hated and feared me. I was the stuff of legend, after all.

The wind battered us as the helicopter touched down, and I saw our Yakuza allies hustle the doctor across the helipad. Ito helped her run while Harada had a box under each arm. Hands in the helicopter reached out to help her in and receive the boxes.

I felt a hand on my arm, and I swung the mace, breaking the grip, and the thing fell back, holding a fresh wound. It staggered, fell, and started dying. The other vampires howled, and three jumped me at the same time. I saw the sky as I fell, and the creatures overcame me. Pain shot up from my legs as they bit down, only to die for their trouble.

Something wrenched the mace away from me, so all I had were my bare and bloody palms, but they would have to do. I struck anything I could see with my open hands, and every hit was answered with a scream. I tried to get up, but the sheer weight of their attack was keeping me down. A boot clipped my temple, and everything went dark as they piled on. All my worries, all my plans, everything I ever wanted didn't matter anymore. The only thought that ran through my mind was, *this is it!*

A scream like thunder pierced through the growling and hissing of the vampires, and I saw the head of my mace swing once, driving three of the creatures away with busted skulls. I blinked and looked at a small, slender young woman in a hospital gown standing on a pile of bodies. Her long dark hair hung in front of her face, but I could still see her eyes wide and wild. Her mouth was open, and another scream of fury sounded.

"Irina?" I mumbled as I stood. I was suddenly glad I opened her cell door before I left the fourth sub-level. She ran to me and grabbed my hand, and I winced with the power of her grip as she dragged me toward the helipad. The noise of the helicopter and the soldiers shooting to clear a path was deafening. I also heard Irina shouting her rage at the vampires, who screamed back. A savage song of hatred.

She kept hold of me and pulled me forward with one hand and swung the mace in mighty arcs with the other. The vampires she hit flew across the helipad, and a few were even launched clean off the roof. Her strength was incredible! It was all I could do to keep up with her. I looked up to see Harada and Ito standing in front of the helicopter, beckoning for us to come. Doctor Kimiko was in the aircraft behind them doing the same. The Americans were using every bullet they had, and their pistols were blazing. Honestly, at that moment…it was beautiful.

The two Yakuza in their suits grabbed the two of us, and we were tossed into the helicopter. They dove in behind us. We started lifting off and then stalled as the remaining creatures grabbed the copter's landing gear, and the weight was preventing us from moving. Shaw and his compatriots were blasting them as fast as they could, and I saw Harada and Ito fighting hard. Irina let go of me and threw the mace at a couple of vampires, knocking them down.

We started rising and rising into the air, and I felt the helicopter pilot bank the machine and increase velocity. I couldn't hear the doctor as she spoke to me over the roar of the engine, but she was wrapping gauze around wounds on my arms and legs. She handed me some headphones for the noise. I was about to put them on when I felt Irina lean against me. Her hands were pressed to her ears, and her face was contorted with pain. For whatever reason, I figured she needed the ear protection more than I did.

I put the headphones on Irina, over her hands, and slowly coaxed her palms away from her ears. When they were settled properly, her facial expression changed. She looked at me with those large, dark, liquid eyes. We both smiled.

The doctor put her hands on my shoulders and shouted over the noise. "Walt! Walt, listen, you've lost a lot of blood…"

Whatever else she said was lost to me as I blacked out.

# CHAPTER 41

A white room. Waking up in another white room? This was becoming a habit. I sat up quickly, looking around. I wasn't back at the facility, but I was in a hospital of some kind. There were a few sensors stuck to my chest, and the bed was adjusted so my head was higher than my feet.

I took off the sensors and looked down. I was wearing a simple hospital gown that was tied in the back and just covered my front. I saw a button on a wire, and it looked like something I should press if I wanted assistance.

Did I want assistance? Yeah, I wanted assistance. I didn't know where I was or where anyone was. What had happened to Irina? I pressed the button and waited. It felt like forever before someone answered.

When the door did open, I experienced a healthy dose of déjà vu. The heels striking the floor, the lab coat, fashionable glasses, and that smile...*Doctor Kimiko*.

"Oh hey!" I called out. "Doctor! You're okay!"

She walked closer and placed a hand on my arm. "Yes, Walt. I am very okay. I am grateful. So many of us are grateful."

"Irina! Is she…is she…"

"Alive and no longer what she was," the doctor explained. "She is no longer a vampire, but she is altered. We are still learning how much and how this could have happened."

I shrugged. "Ah, that would be because of me. I gave her three bags of blood to give her a boost, then I gave her a bag of Harada's blood."

The doctor's eyes widened, and she gave me a hard look. "You did WHAT?!"

"It was a long shot. I had to try."

The doctor walked away from me, biting a nail. "So you allowed her to feed and increase her powers of recovery before administering a dose of Harada's antigens? Fascinating."

I stretched and laid back. "Harada, Ito, Shaw, and the other two soldiers…all good?"

"Yes," she answered as she collected her stethoscope and placed it on my chest. "There were heavy casualties on both sides of the skirmish. Harada and Ito were fine, but the soldiers required bandages and a few stitches."

"The serum you created kept them from changing, right?"

She pulled back the stethoscope and nodded.

"It completely prevented the virus from even starting to reproduce. A complete success."

"Irina, where is she? Where am I?" I asked, sticking a leg out of the bed and shifting forward.

"Patience, Walt," the doctor advised. She went over to a small package and brought it to me. "You are in a hospital in Tokyo. Here are some clothes you can wear. You lost a lot of blood in that battle, but you are well enough to get out of bed."

"Doctor, Irina…is she here?"

She smiled and turned toward the door. "Get dressed, Walt. I will take you to her. She's at the end of the hall."

A few moments later, I was wearing a grey sweatshirt and a loose-fitting pair of jeans. Someone was thoughtful enough to include a belt, so I didn't have to hold them up. A pair of socks and slip-on sneakers completed my outfit. The doctor was waiting outside, and when I came out, she started walking and waved for me to follow.

It was a hospital, all right. Rather plain, and I passed rooms with other patients. I think a few of them were soldiers. Even a few that were Yakuza. The tattoos were a dead giveaway.

We came to a room that had a larger door and a guard. Yakuza, for sure. He bowed when he saw us coming, and we returned the courtesy. He opened the door for us, and the doctor led the way. I craned my neck to see around her.

There she was! It was Irina, but not as I'd ever seen her. Her hair was clean and combed back from her face. She was sleeping, so I couldn't see those beautiful dark eyes. Her breath was deep and regular. Her skin was still pale but nothing like the deathly pallor I'd seen when she lived in cell twenty.

"You're sure she's okay?" I asked the doctor in a whisper.

The doctor also whispered. "She is resting. Walt, she was a vampire for twenty years. Her DNA was rewritten not once but twice! She may look like an eighteen-year-old girl, but she is so much more."

I looked at the doctor. "So what now?"

She frowned. "I don't understand your question."

"Okay," I chuckled. "What are you going to do now? You've solved so much of the puzzle. What will you do with your time?"

She smiled at me. "I have accomplished a great deal. There is still so much research to be done. I know how to treat and prevent the virus that causes vampirism. I also know what your DNA does to anyone infected, but I do not know how it does this. These are not small questions, and they can only be answered in the laboratory."

I turned to face her. "You need to let this go and leave Japan."

"What?"

"Doctor, you've solved the biggest problems

and found the answers that help people. Oyabun wanted the vampires destroyed, and that is essentially accomplished. You have no more obligation to him or the Yakuza. Move on, live somewhere you will be accepted. You deserve no less."

She raised an eyebrow and looked back at Irina. I could tell she was thinking about what I said. "It is something I have never considered. Where would I go? What would I do?"

"Your English is great. Why not America? All the states allow same-sex marriages. Canada does, too," I laughed and shook my head. "You are the woman who broke the vampires and developed a treatment and probably a vaccine. Imagine what you could do if you went after something like cancer? I read they're making big advances with immunotherapy."

There was an awkward silence as neither of us knew what to say. She patted my arm, her way of saying thanks, and turned to face me. "It is worth considering. What about you? What will you do, Walt?"

"I have no idea."

She smiled at me. "I think I can give you some inspiration. We have all the samples we need, and we can replicate your blood, so you are free. Three governments in three different nations have offered to accept you and give you free housing. I also understand that you are to be financially compensated for your contribution. You are a very rich young man. This gives you many options, I think."

I couldn't believe what I was hearing. "What do you mean, 'financially compensated,' exactly? How much money are we talking about?"

She shrugged. "I am told it is millions of dollars. There is also the opportunity for you to travel and provide samples of your blood to different laboratories willing to pay. There is still research to be done."

"Wow...amazing!" I didn't know what else to say.

"There is more," she said, smiling. "Oyabun is beyond grateful to you for saving my life and destroying his enemies. The Yakuza are in your debt. That is no small thing."

This was a lot to take in. I reached a hand out to move some stray hairs out of Irina's face. I stopped just before I touched her and looked at the doctor.

"She took your hand to bring you to the helicopter, remember? There is no danger if you touch her, Walt."

I moved some of her silky dark hair out of her face. To feel the smoothness of her face and the softness of her hair took my breath away. She looked so peaceful lying there. How long would she need? Would she ever completely recover?

"Tell me, Walt. What do you want to do?" the doctor pressed.

Irina took a deep breath and shifted a little in her sleep. I reached out and moved the blanket a little higher on her. "I think I'd like to stay here for a few weeks and then go back to where it all began."

"America?" the doctor asked.

I smiled and shook my head. "Russia. There's something I have to do."

# CHAPTER 42

We had no trouble finding the thick, squat building. Finding my way through Moscow was surprisingly easy. I guess I remembered more than I thought. Memories were coming back whether I wanted them or not.

Seeing the old elevator, the one that looked like a metal cage, was eerie. When I opened the door and heard the rusty hinges complain, I remembered going up to the nice office. When I closed it, I remembered the descent into the basement and seeing my first vampire. I mean, Elena was a vampire, to be sure. But she wasn't old and disgusting. She didn't look like a monster, even though she was.

We walked by Svetlana, who stood up with wide eyes when she saw us. I held a finger to my lips to keep her quiet. "Just wait here, okay?" I whispered, walking a little further up the red-carpeted hall. I took a breath and turned into the open door of the warm office.

Kamenev was behind his desk reading some papers. Wearing his dark suit with the red star on his lapel, he had a pair of reading glasses on and was frowning as he perused the contents of the letter. His dark hair was slicked back, and he had a cup of tea in one hand.

I smiled and called to him as I walked in. "Do you have a moment for an old friend, Comrade?"

He whipped off the reading glasses and looked up. His face broke into a grin. "Walt! I don't believe it. Come and sit, my friend. Take off your coat."

I held up a hand. "I can sit for a moment, but I'll keep the coat. I can't stay."

Kamenev shrugged and gestured toward the comfortable chair in front of his desk. "I will take what time you can give me. How are you, Walt?"

I sat down and shrugged. "I'm good. Really good, but I have no idea what I'm going to do with my life. Not a clue."

He smiled. "You feel like a ship without a rudder, no?"

"I do," I chuckled. "And you? How are things now that the vampires are defeated?"

The Russian held up his hands. "There is still much to do, monsters that must be destroyed, but I have much more time on my hands."

I took a breath and let it out in a sigh. "That's good to hear. You are going to need that time because your job is changing. You have a new job."

He gave me a sideways look. "I do not take your meaning."

I leaned forward in my chair and looked at this man I liked so much. "Comrade, this is going to be very hard on you. It's a lot for anyone to experience. But you've got to understand that it will be every bit as hard on her. You're going to need each other to get through this."

Kamenev stared at me, concerned. "I have no idea what you are talking about."

"I know," I said with a nod. I stood up and walked back to the door. I reached out and took her by the hand. "It's okay. It's going to be okay." I led Irina into the office, and she stopped dead when she saw her father. She was wearing a simple blue dress under her black coat, with matching boots. Her long hair was free. Her eyes were wide, and she was frozen.

The Russian stood up fast and just stared. "*Irina!* Is she…"

I held up a hand to stop him. "She's not a vampire anymore. But she's not exactly as she was. There are memories she is trying to understand, and physically, she is a couple of years older than the day she was infected."

Irina's bottom lip started to quiver, and I saw recognition in her dark eyes. She said one word. "Papa?" Her eyes filled with tears.

I watched the big man in the suit step around

his desk. "Irina? Is it you?" he said in a whisper.

"It's her. It is your daughter," I told him.

Kamenev dropped to his knees. "Irina!" he exclaimed, and he started to cry. The young woman ran past me and dropped to her knees to hold her father, and there was no holding back her emotions anymore. The two of them clung to each other, both crying and trying to speak. Big sobs wracked the body of Irina, and Kamenev kept pawing at his eyes, trying to stop the flow of tears. They held each other on their knees in the middle of the office.

I'd seen everything I needed to see and turned to leave. This was a private moment. It wasn't for me. I wiped at my own eyes as I gained the hallway and approached the secretary's desk. Svetlana's head was down on the desk, and she, too, was crying.

I stopped and put a hand on her shoulder. She reached up and gave it a squeeze. It broke my heart that I couldn't do anything for her. Svetlana's husband and sons were never coming back. I hated that.

I made my way back to the ancient elevator and made sure I didn't go to the basement by mistake. Once was enough. The old machine got me to the lobby, and I walked out into the cold Moscow air. It was refreshing.

Walking down the street, I turned up my collar to the wind and jammed my hands into the pockets of my coat. I felt hot tears running down my cheeks and laughed as I wiped them away with my sleeve. I wasn't embarrassed, and I didn't care who saw.

I was happy. I killed that man's wife, but I did do something miraculous. I brought the man's dead daughter back to him. I gave him another chance to be a father, and she got to be a daughter...and that is a *hell* of a thing!

I laughed as I walked, and the tears started again. Despite all the madness I'd endured, seeing that man hold his daughter made it all worth it. I knew if I never did another single thing with this worthless life of mine, that would be enough.

# CHAPTER 43

A good scarf can make all the difference. A hat can be important, too. Just a few of the many things that a Moscow winter taught me. My bag had a few new books from a small bookstore owned by a charming old man and his wife. They had a great English literature section, and he was willing to get some Russian classics that were translated. Well, he was working on it.

I got to my building and fished for my key. They still hadn't put my name on the directory in the lobby. That was good. I liked being invisible.

This was my new life now. Five months after I was released from the hospital in Tokyo, I had a large apartment in downtown Moscow, rent-free as promised. I took the millions I had been given by three governments and invested it so I would get monthly dividends put into a bank account. I'd use that money to live. Groceries, books, clothes, and a lot of tea. I never seemed to make it as well as Svetlana did. I'd have to ask her secret.

Who was kidding who? I was a recluse now, and I'd probably never drop by Kamenev's office. I was either reading by the fire or walking the streets. Sometimes, I'd get a nice bottle of something with a little kick and enjoy it while I read, but it was usually just walking.

I tried talking with my parents. I really did. They were so understanding and lovely about it all. They wanted me to come home and be with them. But I found I just couldn't talk to them about my experiences. How could I expect them to understand? Who could?

Since there wasn't a support group for teenagers who had blood that was dangerous to mythical monsters, I found myself very much alone with it all. I considered seeing a psychiatrist, but I worried that if I told them the truth, I mean the whole truth, I'd be institutionalized.

I didn't own a television, or even a radio. There was an old computer in my room, but I rarely used it. No social media, just emails. I had no idea what was going on in the real world, and I didn't want to know. I just enjoyed the quiet, the solitude. I needed that.

One thing that did make me smile was the few emails I got from Kimiko. Seemed like something I said resonated with her. She'd moved to San Francisco, was in a relationship, and found a job in a lab. Knowing her, she'd be running the place within a year. She told me that being accepted lifted a weight off her that she didn't know was there. Awesome!

Maybe I was getting ahead of things, but I started to wonder if she would get married. The pictures she sent of her and her partner were terrific. There was something special that they shared. Marriage was certainly possible. I'd made my mind up that if it got to that, I would ask Oyabun to attend the wedding. Doubtful, he'd do it on his own, but he owed me. That would make us even, and I was pretty sure honor demanded that he accept. Kimiko deserved no less.

The stairs creaked as I climbed to the top floor. No elevator in this old building. A beautiful circular staircase was the only way to get home. Some days, I welcomed the exercise. Other days, it felt like too much.

I got to my apartment and used my key in the old brass lock. I pushed open the door, and it was warm. One of the many things I liked about it. For a one-bedroom apartment, it was huge. I suspected it had once been two dwellings, but a wall was removed. The bedroom was a decent size, a reasonable bathroom, but it was the kitchen and living area that I loved. The kitchen was simple but large, and the appliances worked well. It came with a good selection of pots and pans, and I needed that.

While it was nice to cook in such an open and clean kitchen, it was the living room that was my happy place. It had an old fireplace and some nice dark leather furniture. A soft area rug covered the oak hardwood floor. A fleece blanket was on the big chair near the fire so I could cover myself and read by the light of the flames. It was just a great escape from life.

When I wasn't reading or feeding myself, I was cleaning. Maybe it was my time in the facility, but I'd come to value a place that was neat and dust-free. It always made me feel good to come home to a place that was neat, clean, and ordered.

I walked to the bookshelf on the opposite wall from the fireplace and put a couple of purchases in the proper place. The book that was left I placed on the big chair. I would make myself something to eat, get some tea, and settle down for some reading. I know. I was almost in my twenties, acting like I was in my eighties. But it was what I needed, and I always felt better before I went to bed.

There was a firm knock on the door, and I froze. A knock on the door? I'd been there a couple of months, and no one had ever knocked. Not once. Vampires out for revenge? I almost laughed at that stupid idea. Vampires didn't knock.

Again, there was a strong fist pounding on the door, and a male voice called out, "Walt, come to the door!"

Someone knew I was here.

# CHAPTER 44

I opened the door and peeked into the hall. It was a friend, and he was not alone. Ivan Kamenev stood there with a bag of groceries, bread poking out the top, and a big smile on his face. He wasn't in his blue suit, but an ivory wool sweater and a black coat made for a Moscow winter. Behind him stood Irina, wearing a long grey coat and white earmuffs. Her large, expressive, dark eyes looked into mine, and I was lost.

"Oh, wow!" I laughed. "I am so glad to see you. Please come in. I was about to light a fire."

The big Russian moved over the threshold and put a hand on my shoulder. "We will eat, drink, and talk, my friend."

I reached out to relieve him of his burden. "Here, let me take that to the kitchen."

He turned to his daughter and handed her the bag. "Irina has asked to make us dinner. It means a lot to her. Will you allow her to do this?"

She was so beautiful, I thought I would die. Looking at me with those big eyes over the bag of food, asking without saying a word. "Sure, that would be great. Thanks, Irina."

I turned back to the man beside me. "Here, at least let me take your coats!" Kamenev nodded and removed his heavy garment, handing it over while Irina went straight to the kitchen. I heard her set the bag on the counter in the kitchen and come back to me, taking off her coat and earmuffs. I took them and hung them up.

Again, I was tongue-tied just looking at her. "It's...it's great to see you, Irina! You look amazing." I stepped toward her and suddenly didn't know what to do. Shake her hand? Kiss her cheek? A chaste hug? A crisp high-five?

Irina decided for us. She smiled and lifted a hand like she was asking a question. Her fingers were together, and her hand was perfectly flat as she gave me a sly look. I realized what she was doing and put my hand up to mirror hers like we did on the fourth sublevel. No glass between us now. I felt the soft skin on my palm, and we looked at each other. The whole world disappeared. It was just me and her.

She brought her hand down and took a quick step toward me. Looking up, she stole a quick kiss right on my lips and then fled into the kitchen. I stood there blinking, and my hand came up to my mouth. Whoa!

Kamenev called me into the living room. "Walt,

leave Irina to her task. Come and sit with me. We must talk."

I snapped my fingers. "The fire. Let me get that started. Do you want anything to drink? I was able to get my hands on a nice red wine."

"Da! That sounds very good. Bring the drinks and sit with me," I heard him call from the living room.

I walked into the kitchen to fetch the wine, and Irina had already unpacked everything and was chopping vegetables. She meant business. She stopped what she was doing and looked my way as I grabbed the bottle and some glasses. "Walt. I miss you. I miss voice."

I think my heart melted. "I can't believe how good you look, Irina. You're so much better than when we met. I'm happy for you."

She smiled. "I want to talk with you, but father is waiting." She turned back to slicing and dicing.

It was all I could do to tear myself away from the kitchen. I got to the living room and saw that Kamenev was on one knee in front of the fireplace. He had already started the fire. He knew what he was doing. When he stood up, I offered him the chair closest to the fire, and he accepted, leaving the sofa for me. I handed him a glass and turned my attention to the bottle. It opened easily, and I filled our glasses.

He held up his drink. "A toast. To Syn Meduzy!" he said with a wink.

I grimaced, and we touched glasses. "Medusa's

son? Been a while since I heard that little nickname."
We both drank, and he nodded his appreciation.

The Russian looked at me with narrowed eyes.
"Your hair is longer, and you have lost a little weight,
I think. But you look good."

"So, fill me in," I requested. "What's been
happening in the world since I checked out?"

He shrugged. "The older vampires have gone
into hiding, but we are hunting them down and
destroying them. This is going on around the world."

"And the younger vampires?"

"That is much more interesting," he said,
swirling his wine in his glass. "It would seem that many
seek a cure. They turn themselves in, and people use
Kimiko's research to try and rid them of their curse."

"And does it work?"

He looked me in the eyes. "Sometimes. It seems
that the older the vampire, the less chance that it will
succeed. Anyone turned longer than thirty years ago
usually dies."

I pointed toward the kitchen. "Irina looks great.
How is she doing?"

"Ah!" he smiled. "One of the many things I have
come to discuss with you." He took a drink. "Good
wine," he muttered. "My daughter has no trace of the
damnable virus, but it has left its mark on her. Good
and bad."

"I don't understand. What has she been going
through?"

He shrugged. "She remembers her life before the change. Every detail, and she misses her mother. So do I." He took another quick sip and sighed. "It is her memory of her time as a monster that wakes her in the middle of the night."

I sat back in my seat. "My God...she actually remembers?"

"Every victim," he confirmed with a shake of his head. "She tells me that she was out of her mind until she fed, and then there was clarity. At that moment, she would understand what she did. The death of a person or an animal was hard on her." He stopped to gather his thoughts. "My daughter was always headstrong, determined, but she has a very soft heart. These are memories she could do without."

"I'll bet. But physically, is she okay?"

He snorted a laugh. "Better! Her senses are extremely acute, and her strength is extraordinary. It would seem her transformation increased the heightened senses she had as a vampire."

"Really? I do remember her grip when we were escaping the battle in Japan. I couldn't believe the way she swung that mace."

"Walt, she can do things that are incredible. I found your building, but she led me to your door. She did it by scent alone."

I stood up and poured us some more wine. "Okay, that's amazing. Have any of the vampires who were cured shown similar abilities?"

Kamenev shrugged as I sat back down. "Some more than others, but none of them have demonstrated the strength and enhanced senses that Irina has acquired."

I frowned and looked at my glass. "I wonder why?"

"We may never know," the Russian answered with a wave of his hand.

Irina came around the corner and smiled. "Dinner ready. I make you borscht."

"Ah, wonderful, daughter!" Kamenev heaved himself out of the chair, and we all went to the dining table. It wasn't big, but it would allow us all to sit together.

"May I help you set the table, Irina?" I offered.

She scowled at me. "No! You must sit and eat borscht."

Kamenev laughed, and so did I. "Her English is getting really good," I said. "She doesn't have any trouble making herself understood."

"That is my daughter," the man said with a chuckle.

***

It turns out that borscht is a traditional Russian meal. A soup made with meat and vegetables, but mostly beets. Irina was staring at me with wide eyes as I brought the soup to my mouth and blew on it. My first sip was delicious. I looked at the chef and smiled. "Fantastic, Irina! I like this borscht. Or maybe I just like the way you make it."

She beamed at me, reached out, and held my hand. Her little hand was so delicate, but it was warm, and I could feel the unnatural strength. It was there.

Kamenev smiled as he swallowed some of the thick soup. "That brings us to the next thing I have come to discuss with you."

"What is that, Mister Kamenev?"

"Please, call me Ivan." He dipped some fresh bread in the soup as he spoke. "Irina has been going through therapy, learning English, and has decided she loves to cook."

I looked at the young woman holding my hand and smiled. "I think that's terrific, Irina. No wonder the borscht is so great."

She smiled brighter and began to tear up. She wiped her eyes with an embarrassed laugh. "I am glad...so glad you like it."

"I love it," I told her, and shoveled in some more to prove it. I felt her squeeze my hand. We ate in silence for a time. I felt Irina's eyes on me the entire time.

Kamenev was finishing up the last of his bread and soup, and he took a napkin and dabbed at the corners of his mouth. He set his elbows on the table and looked at me with a wry smile. "After everything you have done for us, I am ashamed to say this...but we need your help again, Walt."

Maybe it was the wine or the way he said it. But

I laughed and nodded. "Pretty sure it won't be as hard as the last adventure. Tell me what I can do, Comrade."

He rubbed his hands together. "During Irina's recovery, she had a great deal of trouble sleeping. She woke often and very upset."

I looked at the young woman who was still holding my hand, and her eyes were downcast. "I'm sorry to hear that. It must have been hard on both of you. I'm not sure what I can do to help you with that."

"Ah," the Russian said, leaning back in his chair and tapping a finger on the table. His mouth moved into a wry smile. "Every time she woke, it was crying out for you. She always came out of her nightmares looking for you, Walt."

I looked at the beauty beside me. She squeezed my hand but was still looking at the ground. She started tearing up and wiped at her eyes. Her hand released mine, and she sat there, looking ashamed. It was heartbreaking.

"Oh…I don't know what to say. I'm sorry that I wasn't there for you, Irina."

"No," Kamenev said, holding up a hand. "You were right to give her space. To allow her to be a daughter and me to be a father after so long."

"That was my intention. But I'm still not sure what you're asking me to do. You said you needed my help. Did I hear that right?"

"Yes," he confirmed. "Walt, Irina wants to stay with you. She finds solace in your company, and she seeks you when she is in distress."

My eyes bulged, and my mouth hung open. "What, you mean…live with me?"

He laughed. "I know this must shock you. I truly believe that this will help Irina, and truth be told, I do not think we could keep her from you." He looked around my home and shook his head. "And you, Walt…you have shut yourself off from the world. You need each other, I think."

I looked at the young woman beside me. Her eyes were downcast and moist. It looked like she was expecting the worst. She was nervous.

"And you're okay with this? But…she's so young," was the only thing I could think to say.

Kamenev let out a big belly laugh, and his face turned red. "She was born nearly forty years ago, Walt! She may look like an eighteen-year-old girl, but she is much more. Her life was taken from her for so long. She must be allowed to seek happiness." He looked at me with narrowed eyes. "What do you say? Can she stay with you?"

Irina reached for my other hand, and I allowed her to take it. Her eyes were pleading with me, and I felt my throat tighten. "Yes! Yes, you can stay with me." I looked at her father. "I will be good to her, I promise."

He stood up and smiled at me. "I know you will. She loves you, Walt. That is a powerful thing." The man fetched his coat and started getting dressed.

"It is time for me to leave and allow you to talk of many things." He looked at his daughter and said something in Russian I didn't understand. She just smiled and nodded.

I walked Kamenev to the door, and he shook my hand with a smile. "I have informed my daughter that I will be treating you both to lunch tomorrow. I know a wonderful restaurant, and there is much to discuss."

"That sounds really nice. Thank you."

He turned to go and stopped in the threshold, smiling. "You know, young man, I knew when I first met you that you were important. I had no idea how important you would become. I believe that you and my daughter found more than each other on that fourth sublevel. I think you found so much more."

I watched the man go, and he had a spring in his step as he took the stairs. Maybe it was the wine. He stopped and raised a hand. "I almost forgot! Did you know that Medusa had two sons?"

"No, I didn't."

He smiled at me. "One we do not know much about. The other was Pegasus. The winged horse. That is how I think of you. Where will you fly, Walt?" He winked and started singing a song I didn't recognize as he continued down the stairs.

I closed the door and turned. Irina was walking up to me. Her face was unreadable as she took my hand and led me from the door to the bedroom. She sat on the bed and pulled me to sit beside her.

"When I was vampire, it was like dream," she explained in a whisper. "I remember voice, your voice. I remember your face."

I smiled. "I missed you too, Irina. I wanted to help, and I took a terrible chance. I am so glad you are okay."

She started crying and laughed. "It is hard. When I dream, there is you in dream. When you are not in dream, it is nightmare." She looked at me with those magical eyes, and I caught my breath. "I feel safe with you. I feel good."

I smiled at her. "I feel better when I'm with you too."

She wiped her eyes and smirked at me. She kissed me on the lips gently and leaned back. "Feel good?"

"Uh, yes," I said with a laugh. She joined me and then leaned in again. This kiss was different, and it moved from my lips to my cheek.

I put my hands on her shoulders to back her up for a moment. "Irina, I don't know anything about… about living with someone. It's new to me."

She shrugged. "I do not either. We will figure it out together." She gave me another kiss that lasted. "It will be okay, Walt. Everything will be okay now."

I believed her. At that moment, I believed every word she said.

Author Ian Mitchell-Gill has lived a rich and varied life that made writing almost inevitable. Born overseas and raised in rural Canada, his days were spent playing guitar, engaging in athletic endeavors, and reading every paperback jammed on the shelves. Surrounded by great storytellers in his family and a close-knit group of friends, allowed his imagination to roam.

This path led him down the road to becoming a teacher, and he started writing to create samples for his students to understand how a story is developed and polished. He and his students enjoyed the process so much that he began to write a chapter a week to share with them.

His many experiences and interests proved to be

valuable background for some of the characters and situations in the book.

Ian lives in Oshawa, Ontario, with his wife and two daughters. He continues to teach.

www.ingramcontent.com/pod-product-compliance
Lightning Source LLC
Chambersburg PA
CBHW05073518O626
46814CB00002B/762